To Ty

Red Cell

JOHN KALKOWSKI

Watch out for the football!

John Kalkowski

iUniverse, Inc.
New York   Bloomington

iUniverse books may be ordered through booksellers or by contacting:

iUniverse
1663 Liberty Drive
Bloomington, IN 47403
www.iuniverse.com
1-800-Authors (1-800-288-4677)

Because of the dynamic nature of the Internet, any Web addresses or links contained in this book may have changed since publication and may no longer be valid. The views expressed in this work are solely those of the author and do not necessarily reflect the views of the publisher, and the publisher hereby disclaims any responsibility for them.

ISBN: 978-1-4502-1207-6 (sc)
ISBN: 978-1-4502-1209-0 (hc)
ISBN: 978-1-4502-1208-3 (ebook)

Library of Congress Control Number: 2010901720

Printed in the United States of America

iUniverse rev. date: 03/02/2010

For mom

"The war on terror—it's as much about ideas and creativity as it is bombs and bullets."

—Brad Thor

A cell is the basic unit of life. At its core lies a nucleus, the cell's information center. This contains very precise blueprints that control exactly how the cell functions and reacts to its environment. A mature cell will make room for its life role of delivering oxygen and removing waste by losing its nucleus. Only then is it able to bend and shape itself to channel through the narrowing complex pathways of veins and arteries. By innovating, this free-flowing oxygen-carrying blood cell transforms into the brilliant, deep color red.

Prologue

The dagger-like needle of the scorpion's tail struck.

Its caudal sting criticized the knife blade with a clattering of sharp pricks. Clutched on the rounded end by the sergeant's rolling fingertips, the simple weapon taunted the ancient creature by batting at the strikes with sharp and blunt edges. A single trickle of the syrupy leak clung to the razored edge of the KA-BAR as if begging the sharp point to help carry out the scorpion's venomous will. But this sharp point had specific desires—not merely to punish, but to end.

The small Special Forces unit had parachuted sixty-four klicks south of Ar Rutbah in search of a hidden bunker believed by Intelligence to be the hiding place of the elusive Egyptian terrorist Es Sayid, an enemy so evil that orders had been given for his termination.

The bunker had been incredibly hidden. Delicately carved into the center of a sand dune, it resembled a cave more than a building. It was so perfectly camouflaged in the desert terrain that the sergeant might have completely missed it if he had not spotted the fuel hatch of a mostly submerged gas tank protruding from the dune adjacent to his position. Under dense netting, two jeeps were barely visible.

Entombed in earthen furrows, the unit staked out the perimeter. Smoothed mounds of sand rose like castle walls around them. Wormed into the sand between two of his unit, the sergeant lightly cloaked his body into the crest of the smallest dune facing the bunker.

With a current of vibration, the venom dripped from the knife onto the abdomen of the scorpion now scurrying to bury itself underneath the ripples of sand as if knowing not to waste its hunt on this desert night. Not wanting to share his den, the sergeant stabbed downward, his arm shrouded in a rainfall of earth. The momentary distraction almost proved more costly than the scorpion's potential sting.

The thud of mortar slammed below his sidewall of gravel, hurling the sergeant's body as if a giant sand wedge had gouged him from his pit. Swirls of dust pelted his face. Throbbing convulsions of pain echoed in his head. Sand and dust rained down upon his Special Forces unit like the first shoveled heaps on a lowered casket.

Instinct, pure gut reaction aided by years of hard military training, allowed the sergeant to throw his body sideways and roll straight behind the huge dune closest to the compound as the next wave of shells whiffed through the spot where now only a giant divot lay. Resting his shoulder against the slope of the mound to calm his breathing, the sergeant retraced the splintered remains of fabric once covering the now dented protective plate on his chest. His fingertips cascaded into the folded crevice that had barely blocked his heart from the butchering shrapnel.

Glancing to his right, he could see the injured forms of his weapons sergeant and his communications officer. Sizzling and popping spattered from the destroyed radio transmitter. To his left, the air controller came charging, one hand gripping the starched collar of the squad's intelligence leader whom he drug behind him. Opening his body to the left, the soldier loosely fired multiple rounds at his pursuers.

While diving behind the sidewall, the air controller yelled through exhausted breath, "We missed something." He clutched his left side right above the hip where oozing blood was soaking the earth beneath him.

"Einstein?" the sergeant yelled with concern at the intelligence leader as he rolled over and fired a few rounds from his rifle around the side of the mound. The two soldiers were close. Both had trained furiously together throughout their entire military careers.

Einstein grunted and hunched over, clutching the bullet-punctured remains of his legs. "Prop me up!" he screamed through a rush of pain. Dangerously leaning on the Swiss cheese of his legs, he slumped against the sinking sand.

The shelling had compromised their mission and tilted the odds against them. Without the use of a radio transmitter, they could not call for backup. Handing Einstein his own M-4 assault rifle that still smoked from the just-fired rounds, the sergeant squawked, "A leg for a leg, right?"

Throwing his body forward, the sergeant clawed his way up the slope. He had to act immediately or their temporary shelter behind the dune would be overtaken. His training kicked in. Deciphering information was his specialty. He considered the already memorized layout, noting the positions of the bunker and equipment. Identically angled sand dunes surrounded the entire dugout except for a narrow passageway between them to the very front of the entrance. There appeared to be only one opening.

Outfitted only with his Kevlar vest, a 9-millimeter pistol, and the KA-BAR now strapped to his thigh, the sergeant weighed his options. He couldn't just charge the enemy fire; he would be vastly out-numbered and out-powered. His best chance would be to attack the enemy one by one. He would have to be in close range to fire his pistol, but he wouldn't stand a chance against their machine guns. He would have to remain mobile.

Keeping his body close to the sand, the sergeant crawled to the crest of the dune. Tearing off his Kevlar vest, he ripped open the threaded Velcro. Removing the back plate, he tested it against the sand. Diving forward, he threw his chest onto the smooth ceramic slab and body boarded down the sharp incline.

The two militants charging up the dune had no time to react. As if carving a wave, the sergeant banked sharply in their direction, chunking sand sideways as he hacked the sidewall with hard cuts. The side-to-side motions of his cutbacks made it nearly impossible to be targeted, but it also made it extremely difficult for him to take perfect aim. Missing with his first shot completely, he corrected with a shift of his weight sideways against the plate and managed to re-aim the pistol. Screaming toward the militant's outstretched arm, the bullets amused themselves with the tearing of flesh. Crying out, the man dropped his gun, pleasing the sergeant that he had managed to hit the militant's shooting arm.

Immediately countering with a sharp gouge directly in front of the second militant, the sergeant sprayed a shower of sand sideways into his face. Cloaked in the swell of pebbles was the sergeant's booted foot parting the path of an undone zipper through the tidal wave of sand. With a forcible thrust, the sergeant instantly immobilized the threat by hammering his heel into the man's groin. Drawing his leg back in and leaning his full body weight forward, he burned past this victim and on down the slope. From behind the sergeant came the rattle of the air controller and Einstein's back-up fire.

Rising from a hidden foxhole like the Swamp Thing from his murky depths, another militant rose just meters below him. Nailing the dugout's excavated mound, the sergeant boosted major air up and over the foxhole. A spray of machine gun fire arced into the air following the path of his aerial lift. Executing a perfect "Ollie," he released his left hand from the plate and latched his fingers around the sheathed KA-BAR. Flicking his wrist as he sailed over the militant, the sergeant hurled his knife into the man's stomach, knowing if the knife didn't subdue his enemy, its lethal residue would.

Hurling through the bunker doorway and directly into the sergeant's path, a militant fired his gun at the dropping target. Crashing into a barrel roll with his landing, the sergeant seized and swung the ceramic plate out as a shield with his left hand barely in time to deflect a well-aimed bullet. The force of the bullet's impact spun his body open-faced. Exaggerating the pull with his own ab-flexing twist, the sergeant pivoted and backhanded the makeshift Frisbee, smashing it into the militant's forehead.

At that very second, the slicing, piercing pain of a bullet stabbed through the sergeant's unprotected back, shattering a rib as his body crumpled to the surface. Landing on his side, he could make out the form of a gun-wielding Es Sayid sprinting to the covered jeeps. The sergeant would no longer be able to give chase. He couldn't allow Es Sayid to escape. There was only one option left. He knew he was too close, but he no longer had a choice. Taking what he thought could be his last breath, he locked his elbow and fired a shot straight into the gas barrel.

The explosion sent sand and flames screeching in all directions. The sidewall of the compound exploded into a tidal wave of crusted dirt that spattered the sergeant's flattened body. With reverberating rolls, the shockwave quaked the ground, collapsing the earthen roof and entombing any possible enemy left inside. Igniting everything left unshielded in its path, the exploding jeep buckled in half, sending twisted metal remains and thirty-foot flames licking skyward. Loud hissing came from serrated tires. Once full of air, they were now shredded flaps of rubber scattered across the hardened sand.

The blasting light of the fire scorched the sergeant's sight. Temporarily half-blinded, he coughed and fought to breathe while searing pain tore at his chest. Trying to pull himself upward through a desert grave of sand now covering his body, he found he could barely move. With effort, he shouted over his shoulder, "Einstein?"

In a hysterical sputtering fit of half coughing and half laughter, the intelligence officer yelled back, "I'd say you got more than a leg."

Chapter 1

Top Secret.

The red stamp stained itself diagonally across the manila folder. The warning was clear, though rarely do such furtive things so boldly announce their presence. Yet confidential files as this were not uncommon in this government office. In fact, the man behind the desk where the folder lay might well be asked to review dozens of these in a given day. But what made this particular folder so interesting was that he wasn't examining this one. He was the mastermind behind the project. And by mere notion, it had become classified. It wouldn't just be his reputation on the line if it became public.

Even though he firmly stood by his theory, its contents made him more excited and more apprehensive than any covert operation he had ever been part of. Never had such extreme feelings played tug-of-war with his guts; one moment his stomach would swell with nausea and the next flutter with butterflies and his enthusiasm could instantly condense into cold sweats.

Yet, to the untrained eye, he was a pillar of composure. His finger smoothly traced the rounded edge of the folder's tab as his left hand held steady the morning's newspaper. Crumpled and smudgy under his grip, the paper had aged under his intense stare and scrutiny—he had been clutching the page for most of the morning. If not for the conscious movements of his right index finger, one would think he had been petrified by what he had read, yet his finger easily enough gave away his thoughts. Holding the folded paper open to the third page of the sports section, his thumb underscored the headline, "Injun-uity!"

The article told the story of the thrilling finish for a local Pony League baseball team as they triumphed over a bitter rival the night before. The Chiefs might not have come away with a "W" at their summer season's opening game had it not been for the remarkable quick thinking of their fourteen-year-old star shortstop. Though the Chiefs had been ahead by a run since the fifth inning, the sportswriter noted the deciding play came just moments before the final at-bat.

The night before, during the bottom of the ninth inning, Will Conlan, from his shortstop position, glanced over at the runner on third and calculated how many paces off the bag the guy had stepped for a lead. Digging his fist into the pit of his glove and sweeping the loose gravel with the inside of his cleat, Will readied himself to snag any hit in his vicinity. The opposing Knights had their backs to the wall, and Will figured the batter would be desperate to put the ball into play to try to score their runner. Will hoped Cody, the pitcher, would throw something that could only be chopped for a grounder.

Stepping off the back of the mound, Cody flipped the rosin bag over with a puff of powered dust in his right hand and took a deep breath before dropping it to the ground. Shuffling back up to the rectangular plate, Cody dug his eyes into the catcher's mitt. Kicking his leg high, he let loose with the ball. The second it left his hand, the batter slid his hand down the bat for a bunt. The ball shanked straight and hot instead of down the line.

Will noted that Cody's follow-through had twisted him away from the rolling ball. Knowing Cody might not get to the ball in time, Will charged inward, pumping his legs with exertion. He couldn't simply be a spectator and watch the game slip out of their hands. To Will's right, the base runner was paralleling his dash homeward.

Just as Will was lowering his glove, Cody's hand came out of nowhere, snatched that ball from the grass, and turned toward first base. Bug-eyed, Will wanted to scream. Couldn't Cody see what was happening? Had he forgotten about the man on third? The play was at the plate!

In a moment of panic, he desperately called out to Cody, but the play was happening too quickly. Closing in on the pitcher's mound, Will was badly out of position, but what did it matter now? His head turned to watch the ball leave Cody's hand and, in that split second, Will's vision caught a second spot of white—a pouch that resembled a ball. Obeying his intuitive nature rather than logic, he countered to give his team their only chance. Reaching downward to the incline of dirt, he stretched his fingertips toward the pitcher's rosin bag. In one fluid motion, he seized the pouch and snapped it sidearm toward home plate.

Will saw the watermelon-sized eyes of the catcher swell between the bars of his facemask as he raised his arms to make a target of his catcher's mitt. He snatched the flying object out of the air and slapped his throwing hand inward to secure the cupped object, holding it there behind home plate without another movement of his body.

The runner snapped his head back-and-forth between Will and the catcher and locked his legs, digging his heels into the dirt. Spinning backward, he charged back to third. The catcher didn't give chase.

After a long umpires' conference, the home plate umpire ruled the runner had not been "obstructed" from crossing home plate. Immediately, two screaming coaches stomped toward the home plate umpire. One shouted that the run should count. The other countered that a run couldn't count if the base runner never crossed home plate. Shaking his head, he further contested that there was no specific rule against what had happened. Will watched the umpire shift uneasily from foot to foot as if he were wondering how kids could possibly think of these things.

The man leaned slightly forward in his office chair and rested his forearm on the desk. He had replayed that scene over and over in his mind until it almost seemed as if he had been there to witness it. Clasping a thick sharpie, he drew a red circle around the article. Tapping the newspaper with the cap of his marker, he seemed to make up his mind once and for all. Then, very deliberately, he traced a second circle around the name of the athlete, Will Conlan. Lifting the front flap of the ink-stamped manila folder with the tip of his finger, he slid the article now framed like a bull's-eye directly inside.

Chapter 2

The Giver by Lois Lowry
Essay Response Test #1

Thoroughly answer the following in complete paragraph form:
If terrorism can be defined as "a calculated use of fear against civilians to reach ideological goals," could Jonas (the book's hero) have actually been a terrorist?

Will heard the collective sigh across the classroom as each student completed reading the response question of the now infamous "Mr. Tenepior's Essay Tests." The more thinking it took to answer them, the better. Every kid dreaded them. Eighth grade wasn't supposed to be this difficult.

Ryan, seated in the desk behind Will, muttered, "This is impossible."

Robin, the girl two rows to his right, even started crying silent little sobs, probably because she didn't understand the question. She probably hadn't read the book either. Will could just see her writing about some giant whale.

But, for Will, it was different. There was something intrinsically fulfilling about pushing his mind to find answers. He even slightly enjoyed the challenge. Because this question was not part of the novel's actual story line, requiring it on a test was probably a little unfair for most of the students, but for Will, it fed his competitive nature to prove himself.

Glancing briefly to his side, his eyes found Stacey Chloupek. Even though she was silhouetted against the lone bulletin board emblazoned with the blocked lettering of "THINK," she made it difficult to concentrate. Not only did her long athletic frame drive Will crazy, but her piercing blue eyes added such a depth to her already beautiful face that they seemed to lase rather than look at a person. Her sandy blond hair swayed just below her tan spaghetti-strapped shoulders. She tilted her body slightly sideways and crossed her long smooth legs, sleek enough to accent the mini skirt she wore.

Beads of perspiration started forming on Will's forehead as he watched Stacey lift her pen to her mouth and place its clicker between her sparkling teeth. Obviously pondering over the question before she began, she rolled the pen side-to-side between her finger tips with thoughtful contemplation. Her tongue ever so slightly slid forward and caressed the pen's metal tip. With a sudden jerking gasp, Will lost all control as his head-rested elbow slid off the edge of his desk and his own pen slipped through his fingers onto the floor tile.

"This is a test, Ladies and Gentlemen. We need to concentrate," growled the stern deep voice behind the teacher's desk. Will snapped out of his fuzzy ponderings as he caught Mr. Tenepior's challenging glare. The man shared the frame and demeanor of a Doberman pinscher, Will decided.

Had Mr. Tenepior seen what had happened? He couldn't possibly have known what Will had been thinking. Quickly reaching for his pen, Will exhaled.

Tilting her head, Stacey rested on her elbow as she slouched sideways in her chair. It didn't seem that Tenepior's presence was tensing her.

Shaking his head, Will tried to focus past what normally occupied his thoughts and concentrate on the test question.

Thoughtfully Will gathered his wits. He could easily enough see his teacher's ploy. He figured Mr. Tenepior wanted to see if anyone would be audacious enough to actually agree with his test question. Will guessed that every student would automatically argue the opposite since Jonas had been trying to help his community by giving back the memories and therefore couldn't be viewed a terrorist. Disputing contrary stances on controversial statements like this essay question had often earned his classmates extra credit during class discussions. Supporting the accusation against Jonas would make his essay original and stand apart from his classmates' papers. And Will knew Mr. Tenepior liked that even more.

He slowly put his pen to his paper and began. "It's reasonable to assume that the memories would cause the community fear. After all, the Giver himself described the panic Rosemary's memories caused the community after her release." He paused, letting his mind wander at the possibilities. What he had written sounded just like something Tenepior was after.

"Always support your thoughts with evidence from the text," is what Mr. Tenepior had preached from the very first lesson of the year. That day they had read the short story "Rain, Rain Go Away" by Isaac Asimov. The story described a very odd couple who always seemed concerned with the weather. It turned out they were actually made of sugar and feared being dissolved by rain. By handing out magnifying glasses and stacks of yellow sticky notes to each student, Mr. Tenepior had encouraged the students to decipher clues like a detective. He told the class to question everything they read. "In a short story an author does not have space to waste words. If something seems out of place or unusual, question yourself as to the reason why it's there. There has to be a reason the author used it; you just have to figure out why."

As Will had read this short story, he had torn written notes from his yellow pad and stuck them right in the book along with the words of the story. Clues had started popping out in all directions. After the first few paragraphs, Will's eyes had seemed to sense words floating off the page, standing out as if they had been written in 3-D. It had taught Will not only to be aware of subtleties, but had also helped him clarify the connection of details.

Satisfied he had connected enough similar hidden meanings for his test after twenty-five minutes of writing, he flipped over his paper and glanced around the room to see exhausted students scribbling furiously to finish. A few slackers were slouched backwards playing with their gum and staring off into space. Will was happy that he was one of the lucky ones to have finished such a difficult test. Turning back toward the front of the room, he noticed that Mr. Tenepior had been staring directly at him.

Then abruptly without any warning, Mr. Tenepior announced, "Check over your responses and make sure that you have at least ten specific examples to support your conclusion or I won't accept it as a completed answer." Will knew Mr. Tenepior tailored his lessons to the smart kids, but this was borderline unfair. The test had been hard enough. Any why did it seem that when he finished early, Tenepior instantly added more to it? It wasn't the first time that Will felt that Mr. Tenepior expected more from him.

Chapter 3

"Conlan!" Will knew the voice all too well. Will turned backwards to see Ryan's square jaw moving, "How'd you do?" as he passed his test forward.

Will and Ryan were best friends. Ryan was well liked by almost everyone because of his easygoing, even personality. A sports enthusiast with dark black hair parted to one side and a somewhat lanky yet athletic frame, Ryan played with Will on their select baseball and basketball club teams. Competitive, yet always the good sport, Ryan used his social nature to always be part of the conversation, but oddly seemed too shy to ever ask Samantha, his long-time crush, for a date.

Ryan was one of those kids who liked the sharp look of wearing his jeans with a belt, but rarely tucked in his shirts for anyone to see it. His infectious laugh was readily available, although his smile often skewed into a crooked puzzled look as if he didn't get the joke. Will affectionately considered these inconsistencies in his best friend and liked to tease that Ryan could be compared to "half and half" while Will was naturally "smooth as milk." Even Ryan's scores on Mr. Tenepior's tests demonstrated his "half and half" nature—parts of his essays were marked as clear and concise while others were crossed-out as gibberish filler.

"Dictator Tenepior is going to waste all of us if you don't slow down." Ryan knew firsthand Will's theory about Mr. Tenepior tacking on an extra workload.

Kyle, who had been assigned to collect the papers, had obviously overheard Ryan's comment as he walked down the row. Leaning down so only the two of them could hear, he used his best mocking imitation of Mr. Tenepior. "Will, really stretch your mind here. Will, dig deeper; go as far with this as you can!"

Behind Will, Ryan snickered. Then his eyebrows worriedly rose upward as though he were fretting the awful possibilities of the joke.

Kyle regained his step and strode around Ryan's seat to the next row while keeping his sneering gaze focused on Will. "You need to quit daydreaming about Stacey and concentrate on my class, Will."

"Cut it out, Kyle," said Will as he swatted at Kyle with his rolled-up test. "She might hear you!"

Taking up Kyle's argument, Ryan added, "Hey, if you don't quit staring at her, you're going to kill all of us."

And that's what confused Will the most. Like many in his class, he was a good student. Maybe the top students should be expected to do more. But it was more than that. Did all students have to try as hard as he did? And when did expectations suddenly become demands?

One particular class period where Will found himself surpassing the normal effort curve had involved a writing lesson on the subject of trying to *show* and not *tell* what was happening in a story. Mr. Tenepior had pounded into their brains that they should create inferences for the reader, explaining, "Show smoke; let the reader infer fire." It had become one of his most popular sayings. Mr. Tenepior pushed them to find five examples from their independent reading books and then mimic those examples by writing five of their own. Will cost them five more.

And that was exactly how each class period had been. By having the students read vigorously, Mr. Tenepior spent every day discussing how to develop one's thinking potential. "Let's think outside of the box!"

was one of his most-used phrases, usually adding "Dig even deeper" in Will's direction.

It didn't seem to Will that Mr. Tenepior even cared that the students really learned that much about word acquisition or fluency when they read; he was more concerned with what they could learn from the reading. What new ideas students devised through reading a particular passage seemed to be one of their most common day-to-day activities. Not only did Mr. Tenepior want new ideas to be found, but the more original, the better. He seemed to get particularly excited when a student would come up with some off-the-wall solution to a problem even if it didn't really have anything to do with the reading at all. Sometimes in a fit of excitement he would even take out this awesome iPAQ 210 Enterprise Handheld PC and start recording the conversation or begin typing some notes of the things the kids were devising through their discussions.

One such memorable instance was while they were reading *Fahrenheit 451* by Ray Bradbury. In this futuristic story, the main character, Guy Montag, tries to preserve his people's intellectual creativity by stopping the government from burning books. The government, though, deploys robot dogs to capture Montag. Mr. Tenepior held a contest to see who could draw the best representation of the mechanical hound. After deciding the winner, he reproduced that picture on a series of stickers. To represent how he chased after student's creative ideas, he awarded the stickers to students when they formulated really ingenious thoughts.

Through some off-the-wall connection of the government's suppression of Montag's people, Tenepior somehow managed to tie the discussion to understanding terrorists' oppression as motivation for striking out against America.

Because terrorism was the all-too-familiar topic in the news, Mr. Tenepior tied many of his discussions to some form of counter-terrorism. He particularly made a point of connecting real life experiences like the recent wave of attacks on American soil to the classroom. He constantly assigned the students go to the theater and watch some movie or discuss articles he found in the newspaper about what was happening in the world. Such discussions involved issues like education, elections, gangs, drugs, or even political matters that seemed to be a current hot topic in the news. He would have the students debate each issue, carefully considering all points of view or any, no matter how absurd, ideas that could creatively solve the situation.

That's why it did not surprise Will a bit when exactly one minute before the bell was about to ring Mr. Tenepior announced, "Although your assignment includes reading the first ten chapters of *Holes* by Louis Sachar, we will spend one more class period discussing the novel we took a test over today. In this discussion, we will cover the topic found in your additional second assignment tonight."

An audible groaning gasp could be heard wafting across the classroom. Kyle turned to Will with his eyes crossed and tongue dangling out as he pulled at an imaginary rope above his head.

Behind Will, Ryan muttered, "Man, can't he give us even one break? We just had a test today for crying out loud!"

"Now, now, Class. Do you want me to increase the homework even more?" The muttering ceased almost instantly. Will wondered if it was merely the threat of piling on more work or because Mr. Tenepior had such a commanding presence in the classroom that not even the most unruly kid would challenge him and expect to live. "At 7:00 tonight I want you all to tune into the news program *NewsFocus Tonight.*"

Mr. Tenepior paused as the classroom bell rang, drawing in a large breath and holding it. Although most students began to fidget, not a single student rose from his seat until he was finished.

"The program will discuss a major problem our country is facing that each of us has recently felt the effects of—terrorism. Specifically, broadcast journalists will discuss the topic of how terrorists are defying our nation's agencies by communicating with each other in ways that our country has been unable to detect. After watching this program, be ready to discuss possible creative ways terrorists could be sending messages to one another."

Robin, whom Will considered too sweet to be obnoxious with her question, asked for clarification, "Mr. Tenepior, I don't understand what this has to do with *The Giver.*"

Mr. Tenepior replied, "Robin. Have I not taught you to use your mind? Ask yourself how the Giver communicated the memories to Jonas. Was that not a creative form of communication? Your mission tonight is to brainstorm creative ways such as this that terrorists could be using to transfer plans. Dismissed!"

Chapter 4

Walking out of the classroom together, Ryan said to Will, "Leave it to Homework-by-the-Tons-a-pior to wreck our plans of watching the Cubs' game tonight." Both being huge Cubs' fans had solidified their friendship from an early age as they rarely missed getting together to watch their team play. They had spent many summer days going to Wrigley Field with their fathers in hopes of seeing their team win.

"We'll still watch it," said Will.

Rounding the corner of the school hallway, Ryan grabbed Will's arm and pulled him over to the wall. "O.K., Sherlock. You know that our parents won't allow us to watch until our homework is done. Both programs start at 7:00, so how are we going to manage that?"

Slapping his hand down on Ryan's shoulder, Will answered, "Here's what we'll do. Let's invite a bunch of people from class over to your place to watch the news. During the commercials, we'll turn to the game."

Just then, Stacey and Robin brushed past the two of them. Casting his eyes downward, Will rarely felt confident enough for Stacey's attention after a demoralizing period of Tenepior. It seemed as if Stacey sensed his crush on her and enjoyed seeing him squirm in her presence. Glancing over her shoulder as she walked by, Stacey fluttered her eyes and said, "Hi, Will," stretching out the "hi" to make herself noticeable.

As they passed, he turned and let his eyes follow her tan strides, and continued speaking, "If there are a whole bunch of us, then it will take a fraction of the time to brainstorm together. We'll be done with the homework in no time, get to watch the rest of the game, and have a party at the same time."

"With this big plan of yours and the fact that you haven't yet taken your eyes off her legs, I am guessing you want me to invite Stacey?" questioned Ryan with a sly smile.

"Dad, I'm going to head over to Ryan's house tonight for a few hours. There's a program on TV that I need to watch for class," Will said as he lifted a stack of plates from the table and placed them in the sink.

"This wouldn't have anything to do with the Cubs' game on TV tonight?" his father quizzed with a squinting of his eyes.

"Well, we were planning on watching that after the program Mr. Tenepior assigned us to view. There's going to be a group of us and we all need to discuss it together. That's O.K., right?" Will asked with a faked shyness, knowing his father would be unable to say no because of their shared love for the Cubs.

"Better hurry and finish those dishes then."

At Ryan's home that night, Will found about a dozen classmates scattered around the room, colas in hand. Hanging out at Ryan's house was not a new thing. His parents were very energetic when it came to their kids, often hosting sports club groups, sleepovers, and the occasional school project.

Coming over and pulling him by the elbow, Ryan said, "Will, why don't you take a seat over here." Kyle was watching them closely from the floor and giggling as if some big prank was about to be pulled. "I fought a couple of the guys off to save your favorite spot for you," said

Ryan as he ushered a confused Will over to the middle of the couch. Will could not figure why they were acting so weird.

Sitting down on the brown cushions, Will recognized a particular iPhone encased in a turquoise body skin lying on the coffee table next to the right armrest. Realizing immediately that the joke was on him, Will scooted to lift himself off the couch. Sticking a cold can of Coke into the center of Will's chest, Kyle pushed him back down. "Here's your big chance, Casanova."

Fidgeting, Will shifted his body as he tried to find a position that made him look relaxed and cool like he naturally deserved to be sitting there. With a moist nervousness of his hands, he gripped the Coke as he anticipated the moment with each frantic short breath he took. Not wanting the look of a hopeful tongue-panting dog, he stared down at the couch cushion next to him. In a faked attempt of nonchalance, he picked at a loose fabric thread as Stacey came from the kitchen and sat down beside him. His line of vision was filled by strong smooth legs and secretly he was thankful she still wore the same skirt from school today.

In a relaxed voice, Stacey asked, "Now, Boys, are we here to get this homework done or watch a baseball game?"

Will was at a loss for words. He only knew he would have gladly watched a hundred news programs if it meant spending time so close to Stacey.

"We'll turn from WGN right at 7:00," Kyle replied, indicating that he was just as interested in the game as he was at having an easy way to complete some homework.

Not even looking at the TV, Stacey focused on digging through her purse for something. Slightly discouraged that Stacey didn't seem at all interested in the game, Will silently gave a thankful prayer that at least it meant she wasn't a Cardinals' fan—a fate that could have been disastrous to a hopeful relationship. Barely able to control his racing thoughts, Will couldn't help but breathe in the wisps of her perfume that was making his already tense body even more rigid.

Zipping up her purse, she leaned in toward him. "I'm glad you're here," Stacey whispered into his ear; her breath in his ear tingled his spine. "This assignment should be a piece of cake with you helping."

Delighted by her attention, he could have cared less that she was only after his mind. He gave her a shy shrug of his shoulders and lifted his Coke to his mouth for cover so he wouldn't have to speak with words he feared would come out squeaky.

After a few remarkably awkward silent moments, Stacey continued, "You know, I've watched you play baseball."

Will, knowing all too well that she had been at each of his games, replied lamely, "Really?"

"I saw the game against the Gladiators where you had four hits."

Realizing that she not only knew something about baseball, but had marveled at his hitting ability, caused a surge of icy pinpricks to pelt his body. That's when he realized she had said, "I've watched *you* play baseball" as if implying that she had because of him.

Suddenly as excited as a three-year-old holding a Christmas present, he lost his effort to play it cool and blurted out, "I've seen every one of your volleyball games. That match where you had nine kills was absolutely amazing."

Looking straight at him, she gave him half of a smile like that of a poker player who has figured out another player's hand.

The TV flickered as Kyle changed the channel. The room's chatter hushed as a weathered voice from the TV erupted, "Tonight, a nation in fear." Behind the reporter on a news video screen stood the crumpled wreckage of an interstate bridge. "Striking terror into America's heart on *NewsFocus Tonight*!" The screen faded and was replaced with footage of several successful strikes in major cities across the U.S. The reporter, prefacing with these man-created disasters, shifted his topic to the inability of the National Security Team in preventing the attacks. "We are going to closely examine our nation's ineffectiveness in determining how these terrorists are able to plot and scheme without our knowledge. As we will see, in spite of constant effort to carefully monitor the internet, phone calls, ham radio conversations, and even books checked out from our libraries, our intelligence agencies are baffled as to how terrorists are deploying attacks across the nation so secretly."

The commentator continued exposing all of the communication deficiencies until the first commercial break. Kyle jerked the remote upright and clicked the previous channel button over to the ballgame. With a short top of the inning, the Cubs were already up to bat.

"Good. We haven't missed much," said Ryan to nobody in particular. Will, focusing on trying to hear what Bob Brenly was saying about each pitcher's curve ball comparison, hadn't noticed the slight shift of Stacey's arm downward to the outside curve of her thigh, now gently resting the backside of her hand softly against his own leg.

Brenda, who shared much of the same sharp tone and personality as her big corporate father who worked in the Sears Tower, cut right in, speaking over Brenly's pitching break down. "I don't get it. How does Mr. Tenepior expect us to figure out how they're doing this when our own government doesn't have a clue?"

This time it was Ryan who spoke up, "I think he just wants to test our thinking skills again. It's probably his attempt to make us feel like we're actually discussing something important. Like it matters anyway what we come up with."

"Yeah, I say we just write down a bunch of crazy things like terrorists have gained psychic powers and stuff," interjected Kyle who was always searching for the easy way out.

Will, who had just become aware of Stacey's arm and the warmth of her leg against his, suddenly wanted to prolong the evening as long as he could. He suggested in a slow, encouraging voice, "Why don't we at least finish watching the program in case he asks us specific questions over it."

Kyle, thwarted by a solid opposing argument, replied in an apparent attempt to save face, "Hey, if there's popcorn on the way at this party, I'm in."

The news started up again. More devastating images were displayed. Relieved, Will shuffled his feet nervously against the carpet and tried to act like he was interested in watching the program. Being slightly on edge, he realized how his elbow rubbed against Stacey's bare arm. Its smoothness was about more than he could handle as he became aware of how heavy his breathing sounded and how slowly each second ticked by. Wanting to make his move seem deliberate, yet not be construed as a come-on, he scratched his thigh at some imaginary itch and rested his arm close to hers.

"Commercial, Kyle," shouted Ryan with noticeable irritation as he tried to get him to quickly change the channel back to the game.

Kyle, who had turned to catch the scene with Will and Stacey as it was playing out on the couch, shook his head and flicked the remote. Turning his head again back to the couch, he pulled himself to one knee. Rising, he said, "Anyone need another Coke?" Swaying to the right and passing by the couch, he leaned over and sarcastically whispered to Will and Stacey through the side of his mouth, "I'll bring each of you a Coke so you can stay cozy together on that couch of yours." Raising and lowering his eyebrows repeatedly, he smirked and chuckled to himself as he walked away to the kitchen.

A silent fury passed over Will at Kyle's deliberately drawing attention to every secret longing he had ever had. Not being able to handle the awkward pressure of the moment, Will blurted out, "Hey, it's that shoe commercial on TV—that new shoe that's supposed to be better than Nike," as he luckily noticed the Cubs' game had also gone to commercial.

The wild pumping of his anxious heart mocked his inability to stay cool. Will could feel the warmth of Stacey's hand, and he was sure she could feel his, and yet she had not backed away. Will wondered if she could be sending him a message. Kyle's comment hadn't seemed to bother her, and she hadn't uttered a single come-back, which seemed unusual for her. She was so self-assured that Kyle's weak remark wouldn't have stood a chance against her normal confident rebuttals.

Wondering if this could be the start of the single greatest night of his life, Will grasped at each detail, freezing everything about this moment including the clanging of two ketchup bottles as the refrigerator door opened, how each strand of her hair had a golden shine, and how the gentle breeze of the ceiling fan cooled the heat around his shirt collar. Even the hue of the TV seemed to slow to the flicker of an old movie reel.

On the high definition screen zoomed a marathon runner who jogged down South Franklin Street in his white running shoes as one splashed through a puddle. With his white jersey smearing behind him as he increased his speed, the runner took off soaring up the southeast corner of the Sears tower, hopping between the white-fanged antennas, zooming down the other side, and sliding over the curved ceiling of the lunchbox-shaped atrium with a halt on South Wacker Drive near a parked bus. Giving a thumbs-up sign, he continued to jog off in the distance. Booming, a voice exclaimed, "*Treks!* What trek will they lead you on? Coming soon to a store near you."

From over his shoulder Ryan jeered, "Maybe a pair of those shoes would help you steal bases better, Will."

Wondering if Ryan was actually talking about baseball or his current situation on the couch, Will took a second to recharge his wits. "Well maybe if you would get a hit now and then, I wouldn't get thrown out trying to steal second."

From the floor, Kyle cracked, "Aw, shut up. You both know the only time you ever score is when I hit a home run."

Before Will could even open his mouth to reply, Stacey drew in a breath and slyly called out toward Kyle without skipping a beat, "You strike out in baseball almost as much as you strike out with the cheerleading squad." The eruption of laughter throughout the room fizzled Kyle's steam. Seeing how she could play it cool in far more than English class, Will reached for her hand. Not sure if he simply thought the moment was screaming for boldness or if he simply couldn't resist her any more, he took the risk and entwined his fingers in hers.

Stacey looked down at the coupled hands and up at Will. "Your hand is very warm." Although normally that directness would have embarrassed him beyond belief, he didn't care—she hadn't let go.

Will found his attention to both game and news program fading as, slowly at first and then gradually becoming easier, Stacey and he began a conversation. Rarely adding to the conversation in the room, Will was barely aware of the game's score.

"So how come you never asked me out?" Stacey pointedly asked.

Pondering his possible responses, Will replied, "I was kinda hoping you'd let me do that now."

As if she had been in full control of the situation all along, Stacey merely sat on his statement, forcing Will to spit it out and physically say the words aloud. As a second passed, she drew her tightened lips sideways and raised her eyebrows toyingly.

As her cute sparring continued, Will slowly regained the smoothness he showed on the baseball field and Stacey served an ace now and then that made Will more certain each time of her absolute perfection. The end came all too quickly when everyone got up to leave. Will hung back, trying to stretch this perfect evening even longer.

"So much for your help," said Ryan as he came over to the couch after saying bye to everyone else. "You know, usually when someone wants to have a study party, they typically help do some of the work."

"Sorry," they both replied in unison, smiling at each other as if it were a sign that they were a natural match.

"I feel like I did half the work myself. Did you guys hear anything we talked about?" Grinning, Will looked downward and played with the corner of the floor mat with his foot.

With a sigh and a roll of his eyes, Ryan said, "I'm going to have to cover for you both tomorrow in class, aren't I?" Nodding yes, Will felt slightly ashamed, though he knew his friend was actually happy for him and would be glad to do so.

"Things went O.K. tonight for us," Ryan pointed out, "but knowing your history with Mr. Tenepior, I doubt tomorrow will be all that smooth for you."

Chapter 5

Will woke up the next morning feeling like he glided through the air, not caring if Mr. Tenepior yelled at him the entire class period. He had spent the most perfect evening of his life with the girl to whom his heart had been dedicated for as long as he could remember. He just hoped it hadn't all been a dream.

"Morning, Champ," his father said at the breakfast table as he peered over his newspaper. With a clearing of his throat, he added "Lucked out last night, huh?"

"Lucked out?" Choking and holding his fist over his mouth, Will looked toward his dad to see if he knew about last night with Stacey, but his head was studiously tucked between the folds of the newspaper.

"That was a heck of a homer to end the ninth," his father replied.

Tearing the sports page from his dad's hands, a relieved Will picked his way through the headlines exclaiming what a big win it had been.

A puzzled curve of an eyebrow signaled his dad's bewilderment. "Is there something going on here that I should know about?"

Forgetting completely about the game, Will realized now that last night couldn't have been a dream. Stacey was probably the only thing that could divert his attention from a game. "Ah, well," he started, figuring his parents were going to find out anyway. They teased him about Stacey on a regular basis. "The Cubs weren't the only ones who hit a home run last night." A grin pushed its way to the corner of his cheek.

"Holy cow!" his father called out in his favorite Harry Caray impersonation, "Mother, I think Will has something to tell us."

"What is it?" she asked, rounding the corner to the kitchen.

"Our son, here, doesn't seem to know that much about last night's game. I wonder what could possibly compete for his attention more than that?" His parents looked at each other and then turned their attention back to Will.

"Who all happened to be at Ryan's last night?" his mother questioned with an innocent raising of her eyebrows.

Guessing that they had already figured it out and were just messing with him as they usually did when it came to his crush on Stacey, Will decided to tell them that he had finally asked her out.

"Well, that must have been quite the study party," his father surmised.

Will just smiled widely as he looked back down at the paper. Recounting the division standings, an article summarized that the Cubs were neck and neck with the Cardinals with not quite two weeks left in the regular season. Needing to win this series to put them in the lead of the National League Central Division, the Cubs were facing another chance at the playoffs. With delighted satisfaction, he folded the paper. He decided nothing could ruin this day, except, maybe, English class.

The day couldn't have gone more smoothly. He had eaten lunch with Stacey and talked to her between every period in the hallway by her locker. With something to think about other than what his teachers were saying, his classes had flown by. He now had only one class left, one he wished he could skip.

"Alright. Thinking caps on. After viewing the news program, what did we come up with?" asked Mr. Tenepior, seizing the chance to start the period off brainstorming. Students began raising their hands immediately. Will knew that everybody in class realized Mr. Tenepior seemed to go easier on those who volunteered. "Kyle, since it's so seldom we see your hand raised, we'll start off with you. May I add that I am impressed with your fervor?"

From the front row Kyle had been waving his arm wildly right under Mr. Tenepior's nose. "Um, yeah. Lots of us got together last night to discuss this."

"Is that so? I like your initiative," replied Mr. Tenepior.

"Yes. Like I was saying, I don't think the government has examined the possibility of telepathic powers," Kyle continued with a completely straight face. "No one would be able to detect that." As if adding an exclamation point to his reasoning, he tossed his moppy blond bangs to the side with a fling of his neck.

"I see. An interesting place to start. One cannot dispel even the most unlikely possibilities without a shrewd examination first," replied Mr. Tenepior. "At least your thoughts are not contained by a box."

After a brief hesitation and counter flip of his note pad, Mr. Tenepior continued, "Remind me to come back to that thought later. It really ties well into our reading of *Holes* for today when Stanley reasoned that the shoes simply fell from the sky."

Will realized that through simple diversion, Mr. Tenepior had skillfully danced around wasting class time discussing such a preposterous notion as Kyle's without condemning imaginative thinking.

Satisfied, Kyle nodded his head and jutted out his chin smugly as if all this brainstorming work was child's play to him and he had successfully done his part.

After Mr. Tenepior had sorted through several theories and entertained a few other conclusions, Ryan took over, discussing internet possibilities. "The show last night discussed how some terrorists had e-mail accounts that were untraceable because they only saved drafts of e-mails."

Brenda cut in to add further explanation, "By sharing the account's password, they didn't have to send out e-mails that could be intercepted and viewed by our government."

Butting back in, Ryan offered, "Why couldn't they still be doing this? It worked in the past."

Although Brenda and Ryan's back-and-forth offered interesting discussion points, Will hadn't participated until five minutes before class was over when Mr. Tenepior detoured and directed his attention toward him. "Let's see. Will, we haven't heard from you yet."

From where he had sunk deep into his seat, Will gripped the side corners of his desk with white knuckles. Will had been dreading this moment, but he had been contemplating a plan he hoped might work. "I had the same ideas as what Ryan said earlier. Some of us worked together last night."

Will knew Mr. Tenepior was not one to be fooled. "You've heard me say before that voice is one's personality put into words," Mr. Tenepior thundered. "And as an English teacher can easily point out, there wasn't a single proposal that sounded of your voice, Will."

Will knew Mr. Tenepior had grazed over each and every word he had written this year and conversed with him during every discussion. Will knew that both Mr. Tenepior and he recognized that none of the ideas heard today were his. None of them even sounded remotely like what he would have answered. How could he argue with that?

"Mr. Tenepior. Truth is I did watch most of the program last night, but I got too busy to come up with any new ideas." Wrong word choice. Busy. Mr. Tenepior would know that he was with the group. If he had been too busy, then what was the rest of the group doing? So he quickly added, "Not too busy, I mean, I just didn't feel like it."

"Why not? Isn't our nation's security a concern for you? Don't you want to feel safe?" Tenepior punctuated his loud, disgusted comments by waving his arms in wide circular motions through the air.

"Great, leave it up to Tenepior to go global with his hazing," thought Will. He lowered his head to stare at his desk and did not reply. This obviously infuriated Tenepior.

"This lack of effort does not belong in my classroom!" he yelled, stabbing his finger at the desktop and glaring into the eyes of all his students making the point clear to everyone that he should not be crossed. He inhaled, expanding his chest into an inhuman shape. Will knew he was about to explode. "Will. This is what you are going to do. Listen closely. There will not be another chance." Slowly exhaling snorting breaths through his nose, he directed, "You will use every ounce of your brainpower to cultivate one plausible theory that answers this assignment. You will show all possible steps necessary to enact this very scheme. You will consume yourself with the task in a twenty-five page research paper. Document all resources you end up using. You will not pass this course without my 100 percent approval of your conclusions. Do I make myself clear?"

"That's going to take some time," squeaked Will, not wanting the wrath to come down on him again.

"So be it. Have it on my desk no later than two weeks from today," Tenepior affirmed with staunch gruffness. His eyes scanned the rest of the room, obviously making sure that his points had sunk in for the rest of the students, and added, "Anyone else this includes?"

Will quickly strained for his attention to divert it away from Stacey, "It was only me. I goofed around while everyone else was working."

Will figured that Mr. Tenepior was too sharp not to see through this lie, but he seemed to disregard the response and let it pass. It was as though Mr. Tenepior wasn't really concerned with anyone else, but, for some reason, was determined to get what he wanted out of him.

Chapter 6

The next two days that finished off the week had gone about how Will had expected. He went to school, came straight home, closed the door to his room, and worked on the paper he now owed Mr. Tenepior. There was little time for much else. Even though the assignment left a bitter taste for Will, he couldn't help but somewhat feel that it was all still worth it.

After Mr. Tenepior called his parents and told them the situation, Will was grounded. Will was especially pained after learning he, as part of his punishment, wouldn't be allowed any social opportunities until he finished his research paper.

Even though Will understood his parents were sticklers about his getting his work done and definitely would not put up with his disrespecting a teacher, his parents allowed Will to negotiate one fortunate compromise. Will bargained with his father to allow him to watch the Cubs' game that Sunday night at Ryan's house since it was the start of the last home series of the season if he completed at least the first fifteen pages of his report.

By late Sunday afternoon, Will came down to the den to show his work to his father. "I've got nineteen and a half pages done." He handed his father the sheets of paper.

"So you're going to be able to finish sometime early this week and turn it in before it's due?"

"That's my plan," Will fervently stated, knowing the sooner he finished, the sooner he could start spending time again with Stacey. It had been the real driving force behind his work ethic. "The game's about to start, so I'm headed over to Ryan's like we agreed."

"There's not going to be a bunch of people there tonight, is there?" his father asked, looking above the rim of his reading glasses.

"Just us. See you," called Will as he left.

Seeing Will come to his door, Ryan asked, "So you got it done, huh?"

"Almost. Did I make it in time?" Will headed for the couch. Breathing a deep sigh, he felt like melting into the couch after working so hard the past few days. His mind needed a break. The game would be perfect for that, except the importance of the game added a whole different level of stress for Will.

Will anticipated that the final four-game series versus the Houston Astros would make for an exciting finish since Houston was having a great season because of their strong defensive play. By the bottom of the fourth, though, the Cubs had destroyed that reputation with a five-run inning, three of them unearned.

Ryan, sliding onto the couch next to Will, exclaimed in exasperation, "Wow! The Cubs never get breaks like that. It has to be their year."

Nodding his head Will turned in agreement, "I sure hope so." Gazing back at the tube, he saw that commercials were capitalizing on the team's success.

"Hey, there's that Treks shoe commercial again. Dad said I could get a pair for basketball season if they're out by then," informed Ryan. Though this wasn't the same ad that had played earlier, seeing the commercial made Will think back to Wednesday night with Stacey.

The TV screen zoomed out from Ron Santo's flag flying over the left field wall of Wrigley Field and focused on the green scoreboard in center field as a rectangular opening appeared and a yellow three number board disappeared. Through the opened slot crawled an almost completely naked streaker. Wearing only his Treks sneakers and a blurred haze over body parts, he landed on the center field enclosure and jumped over the bushes below. Bounding over the wall, he started racing around the bases as the crowd sang "Take Me out to the Ballgame." Using the trusty traction of his shoes, the runner leaped over umpires and dodged field workers as he sprinted to the right field wall. He scaled the ivy, soared above the bleachers, and dove over the outfield wall onto Sheffield Avenue. Standing in the wake of the right field foul pole, he flashed a thumbs-up sign and sprinted away. Once again the same robust voice boasted, "*Treks!* What trek will they lead you on? Coming soon to a store near you."

Just as the commercial ended, Ryan's father came into the room with news, "I've got a surprise. Dennis Worthy from the bank just called and said he had four tickets to the game Wednesday night if you boys would like to go. Will, I called your dad already and he said that he couldn't make it and he wasn't so sure you would either. He said something about work that you had to finish first?"

"No way! Sure I want to go. Don't worry about the work. I'll get it done. There wouldn't be a chance in the world I'd miss that game."

"Dad, you said you had four tickets?" piped up Ryan.

"I'm sure we can find someone to go with us. Or we could always get rid of it easily enough at the game," replied Mr. Moritz.

"Hey, Will. Why don't you ask Stacey to go along? It'd be a nice way to make it up to her for not being able to do anything the past week. Would that be alright, Dad?"

"If she wants to go, that'd be fine." Lowering his hand from the door frame, Ryan's dad turned to watch the game in the other room.

Now more excited than ever, Will asked, "Ryan, do you mind if I use the phone to call and ask her now?"

"What do you think? Remember, you owe me big," teased Ryan. Ignoring the direct order of his parents about lying low on the whole Stacey matter for the duration of his grounding, he reached for the phone.

A half hour later, Will was still giggling and chattering loud enough to drown out the play-by-play of the broadcast. Shouting over the nonsensical babble, Ryan groaned, "Should I be worried about what I've gotten myself into?"

Will replied by rolling his eyes.

"So do you like me more than volleyball?" Will asked Stacey in a sheepish giggle. "How about more than shopping for new clothes?" And then after a several-second pause, "Do you like me more than volleyball and shopping put together?" Will absentmindedly played with the end of his shirt with his fingers as he slouched in the recliner, the cordless phone pinched between his ear and shoulder.

But it wasn't until Will replied, "Yes, I like you more than the Cubs" that he noticed Ryan stand up and punch the volume button on the remote to such a level that the walls began shaking with vibration. Cupping his hand over the phone, Will lent Ryan his ear.

"Wanted to let you know that you're missing a great game, Man."

Chapter 7

Will tugged his sheets all night long as his mind busily replayed highlights of the night's big win. It was hard to sleep knowing that the final regular season game he was going to the next evening would decide the Cubs' playoff future.

He couldn't help but think, as his head also fought against the lump in his pillow, that the success of the evening might also clinch his playoff future with the girl he was absolutely mad about. Finally, he shuffled his feet to the shower and then his computer. He might as well put those swirling thoughts to use.

While numbly pounding out paragraph after paragraph on his computer, he quickly added pages to his report. He felt confident that Mr. Tenepior would like his proposal. He thought it unlikely that terrorists were actually meeting face-to-face. Traveling would leave records—records of gas stops or plane flights. If they had innocent people doing the traveling for them, then there was no trail to follow.

He had heard of drug smuggling stories where illegal drugs could be hidden under vacationers' vehicles and when they headed back home down Interstate 80, drug smugglers on the other end would wait for travelers to return and search their cars. Why couldn't a similar theory work for terrorists?

Thinking back through all this made him uneasy. Considering the recent attacks that he had researched, he couldn't understand why people would want to cause so much pain and suffering, especially to innocent people. It would devastate him if one of their attacks harmed his mom or dad or Stacey. He arched his back with a huge yawn. Bending back, he could feel the rumbling and gurgling of his stomach and decided it was time to eat some breakfast.

He had been in too much of a daze to talk over all the game's highlights with his father when he had returned home last night, so he was anxious for their morning chat.

Gripping the handle of his coffee and slowly taking a sip, his father greeted him. "See you're up early this morning."

Grabbing a day-old sugar doughnut from the counter, Will, feeling a bit dizzy, leaned over to rest on his elbows. Taking a bite, he said, "Wanted to get some more of that paper done. Couldn't sleep." The doughnut stuck to his throat as he shoved half of it into his mouth.

With a knowing look his father stated, "Thinking too much about Wednesday night."

Suddenly his stomach lurched. Will doubled over, wrapped his hands tightly over his mouth, and made a dash for the bathroom. Though quick to his feet, his father was too late to help. Some deep intuitive worry had sunk to his gut. As if the stress from his assignment was acting as a self-preserving reaction, his stomach was complaining to Will's whole body that something just wasn't right.

His mother leaned in toward the bathroom door, "Are you sick, honey? Is it something you ate? It's all that pop and popcorn and sugar you had last night. I know it is. Do you need to stay home from school today?" his mother rattled away hurriedly, making Will's stomach churn even more.

Dragging himself back to the kitchen, Will felt a little better. Needing to get some food in his belly, he eyed the doughnut again. Breaking the leftover portion into three pieces, he popped one into his mouth. Missed flakes of powdered sugar hung loosely at his upper lip. With so much going on in his life at the moment, he wasn't sure what had caused his sudden queasy feeling.

"Too much on your mind. Maybe we should cancel your going to the game this week. You've worked so hard on that paper, and with all the excitement you've got right now..." Will's dad paused, then added with a stern look of his eye, "It might do you some good to stay home for once."

"I'll be fine, Dad. Just let me get this paper done." It had sounded like the right reply, but for some reason he couldn't shake the nauseous feelings rising inside him. It was an ominous way to begin the morning.

Usually the start of Will's school day was a complete waste of time. He normally resented having study hall first hour. In his opinion, whatever administrator thought that it would be a good time to schedule one wasn't thinking straight. Of course it was good for a lot of the slackers who waited until then to finish all their work. But for Will, who had parents who forced him to have all his homework done before he could do anything else, it had been a boring way to start each day. Today, though, he was thankful for the time. He only had a page and a half to type and the fifty-three minute period would be just enough.

As the period was coming to a close, he wrapped up his essay. Going over to the printer to grab the final pages, he looked for a stapler to use. At that moment the high screech and crackle of the intercom clicked on. A slightly tremulous voice of the secretary requested, "Mary Jean Allison, Paul Pankonan, Alice Walters, Bill Shulte, and Lisa Erickson, please come immediately to the office."

Clanking his set of papers against the table to make sure all were in line, he raised the stapler to the left corner. He glanced up to the clock to see how much time he had left to spare. With the period ending at 9:16, he still had a few minutes left.

Once again the fuzz of the intercom sounded, "I need also Brenda Rodgers and Brad Smith. Come to the office, please."

"Holy cow. What's going on?" said an excited Ryan shuffling over to the printer where Will still stood. "Brenda never gets called to the office."

Just then, through the windows of the media center doors, Will saw Mr. Tenepior sprint past, stretching his arms through his jacket as he ran. More announcements blared from the speaker. Will, suddenly reliving the queasy feeling in his stomach, walked over to the study hall supervisor who was oblivious to anything but writing out hall passes. Will asked her, "Mrs. Stevens, would it be O.K. if I turned on the TV in the corner for a second to check the news?"

This time from the loudspeaker came the voice of the principal. "Teachers, please keep your students in first hour until further notice."

With a groan, Mrs. Stevens looked up at the clock, bags sagging under her eyes. "Will it keep the two of you quiet for the rest of this time?" She nodded to Will. "Just make sure the volume is set low."

Ryan followed as Will reached up to press the power button. "You think something's going on?"

The TV sparked to life. Grey billowing clouds roaring through aluminum window frames appeared on the screen. Suddenly zooming out through a whirlwind of loose papers, the image showed broken tree trunks and crumpled light posts toppled onto each other like dominos. Police sirens blared, and dust-covered fire fighters ran in all directions carrying fire hoses and patting down burning victims. Rubble of red granite slabs and black glass was strewn across the pavement. Dust pelted overturned vehicles like a thick sleet on a winter day. Suddenly a breeze cleared the way; a perfect view of what unmistakably had to be the Sears Tower loomed above the wreckage below. Though the tower itself was still intact, the first ten stories had been hollowed like a parking garage.

Will knew this had not been some simple fire. No fire could have left debris such as this. It had to have been a bomb.

Chapter 8

Will continued to stare at the television as Ryan shoved his cell phone in front of Will's face. "Check out this text from my mom. Your dad's coming to pick us up."

"No way! We're leaving school?" Will asked as he read the message.

"Doesn't look like it's just us," Ryan replied as he nodded toward the line of students at Mrs. Stevens's desk holding out their own cell phones and asking to go to the office. "My dad will come pick me up from your house when he can. Mom's on her way to hear the mayor speak."

That didn't surprise Will at all. He had pieced together that this would be among the busiest days for Ryan's newspaper reporter mother. Sitting down to wait for his dad, he watched as parent after parent flooded the hallways. It seemed to him that his school was as much a flurry of activity as the lives of reporters were.

Over an hour later, Will was relieved to have finally made it home through awful traffic. Flopping down on the couch, he glued himself to the TV. As he guessed, Chicago, seeing its first large-scale act of terrorism, was in disarray.

Locking down, the city canceled all flights, and most businesses closed shop. The ticker scrolling across the bottom of the screen had told that all metro schools had closed shortly after 10:00 that Monday morning. Video clips showed police cruisers swarming the streets as additional security came from all across the city and neighboring suburbs. News reporters gathered along Adams Street, outnumbering the police three to one.

Mostly unscathed, the Sears Tower, wearing its dreary black shroud in mourning, still loomed over the city. Its bottom floors, crumpled and shredded, had ruptured like a worn-out shoe. The once glamorous lobby, now disfigured and beaten, marred its foundation like varicose veins. Being the engineering miracle of bundled tubes that it was, the tower had not collapsed. The footings and frame still remained strong after taking the blast head-on. Around window corners, smoke smeared streaks of thick sooty eye liner. For the most part, only windows had been shattered. Nearly a hundred stories had been unharmed. But little did any of this matter. The people whose lives were lost could not be replaced.

One female reporter's voice told the story serenely as if giving a funeral eulogy. "A sad day for Chicago. A sad day for the nation." Brushing dust from under her eye she continued. "9:00 this morning at the very start of a busy work week, time stopped. The rise and fall of car engines, the muffled trampling of feet on the sidewalk, the flickering of stop lights were all halted by the blast of a car bomb. A blast hurling a destructive wave through the Sears Tower. A blast whose tremor could be felt in the pits of our stomachs."

Will and Ryan had not been able to take their eyes off the tube. With an unlocking of their front door, Will's mother staggered in. Stretching her lips into a horror-stricken grimace as she once again saw actual camera footage, she muttered, "Oh, my gosh." With her hand outstretched over her gaping mouth, she stood as transfixed as they were.

Sharing a similar expression, the reporter continued. "Directly behind me on Wacker Drive once stood the vaulted atrium that welcomed enchanted tourists for their visit. Beside it were two parking lanes etched into the pavement for viewers arriving by bus. But today, tragically, that's not all that arrived by bus." With short breaths, she went on to describe how a bus transporting explosives pulled right up to the doors of the tower and exploded, creating the disaster of the footage they had been viewing all morning.

Will's mother, still too shocked to really speak, kept muttering "Oh, my gosh."

The reporter explained that casualties were yet unknown, but previous estimates had been in the low hundreds. No specific terrorist group had claimed the bombing.

As Will listened to the reports, he couldn't shake a feeling that had bugged him all day long. A crystal clear image of the tower seemed so fresh in his mind even though he hadn't been there for quite some time. In fact, it startled him that his memory distinctly picked out the sharp half-hexagon angles of that very bus lane cut away from the street, though he wasn't particularly aware of ever noticing them before. It just seemed so familiar, almost like déjà vu.

Breaking Will's concentration, it was Ryan who unwittingly made the connection. "I wonder if the game will still be on TV tonight."

"Jeez, I sure hope so," spoke Will who was now considering the possibility of everything becoming ruined because of the attack. "Dad, turn to ESPN to see if they say anything about the postponement of games."

Though Will knew baseball seemed of little importance compared to the loss of life and destruction that had occurred, his father surprised him with his response. "I agree. We need something a little more hopeful for a change." He lifted the remote to change the channel.

"Pardon the Interruption" was well underway, displaying a red sidebar full of topics all dealing with the catastrophe in Chicago. Scrolling to the next headline reading "Comish," Michael Wilbon transitioned, "Just minutes ago the Commissioner of Baseball, siding with the Commissioner of the National Football League, had this to say…"

The TV screen transferred to a video clip of a press conference. A tall man stood behind a podium crowned with batches of clipped-on microphones. "Today our hearts go out to the citizens of Chicago. Though baseball can be a sport of bitter rivalries often pitting one city against another, tonight we will look to our great sport of baseball to help us unite together and remember there are great things to enjoy about our way of life. Just as a difficult decision was made to continue major sporting events after the attacks of 9/11, tonight's games will be played as scheduled. We will not let these cowardly acts, aimed at making us fearful, tear us down!"

An "Oh, my gosh," flared from his mother again.

With a pained rub of his balding head, Tony Kornheiser added his assurance, "It's a courageous move for the commissioner to make such a decision, one for which he may be criticized. And I feel way down deep in my gut that he made the right choice."

In agreement that the games should continue, both commentators pointed out that sports had helped people add some normality to their lives after 9/11 as the commissioner had alluded to.

At one point, with an emphatic wave of his hand, Wilbon, a proud Chicago native, shouted out, "This is America, and nothing represents America better than its own national pastime. Baseball holds the hopes and dreams for so many people at a time when we all especially need to feel these for ourselves. I know the people of Chicago live for this sport. It is essential that baseball continues."

For the first time that day since completing his paper, Will felt a spark of fire burn inside him. This made him feel proud. As excited as a child on his birthday, Will eagerly awaited the night's game. He felt that if he had the chance to step into the batter's box, he could hit a home run. With all of this and the playoffs in hand, it would be a game to remember.

Getting up to help prepare dinner before the game, Will walked to the kitchen. By grilling some hamburgers and setting the table, he helped his mom while occasionally taking a second to tune in to the kitchen TV where the news coverage continued. He listened as one analyst after another reported his theory as to why the attack had occurred and why the Sears Tower had been chosen. He watched as heroic rescue workers scrambled frantically to aid the suffering who had been scathed in the explosion and as investigators poked through the debris searching for clues.

As the night loomed closer, reports started shifting to how fortunate it was that more damage had not been done. A WGN news analyst reported, "A security measure taken after 9/11 to ensure the safety of the tower seemed to have offered substantial resistance to the attack."

Reporters described embedded concrete flower planters placed street-side around the tower that had prohibited the vehicle from coming into contact with the building. They theorized that the loading dock had not been the point of attack, probably because of its explosive detection systems.

Reporters speculated the attack had not occurred as planned. One reporter stated, "The information police have collected primarily shows that this incident could have been a lot worse. Ground Zero for the explosion was just beside the American flag pole in front of the plaza steps. The police suspect that the bus was unable to pull as close to the building as it had intended, probably some two hundred fifty feet further from the doors than what most likely was their target.

"The surveillance cameras showed three buses back-to-back directly in front of the atrium's entrance already occupying the northern bus area. The buses containing *Midplains Tours* vacationing groups arrived a half hour earlier than scheduled. Two more touring buses were parked in the southern-most bus lane when the bus with the bomb pulled in. The Tower's intelligent video systems searching for anomalous vehicles sent a security officer to question the last bus when the bomb suddenly detonated. Among the many suspected casualties from this incident included those traveling with the tourist company. A fate whose loss is unimaginable. A fate that may have saved the Sears Tower."

Will jerked his head backward to hear his mother's words that had not been spoken, but an "Oh, my gosh" would have been appropriate.

"I can't stomach any more of this. Let's see if there's anything good on ESPN. They might be showing some pre-game," suggested Ryan.

Turning channels, but not seeing anything about the game, Will decided they should go ahead and eat while they waited for the game to start.

As Will ate, he couldn't help but pick at his food a little. Something pried at his insides about the bombing that had taken place that day. Yes, he felt compassion for those who were suffering or even dead because of this, but that was not what kept giving him the uneasy notion prying at his brain.

Images kept flashing before his eyes: the first glimpse of the rising smoke from the TV, the Sears Tower standing so tall and seemingly unconquerable, Mr. Tenepior racing through the hallway. He felt that there was something more to all this that he alone might be connected to—something that said he should have seen this coming.

Chapter 9

School was canceled for the second day in a row. A sad hollow feeling still possessed Will. Never had he thought that his life would be affected by such an incident. He had assumed that these things always happened somewhere else—someplace he didn't live. And why did he feel such emptiness inside? His life wouldn't be that different because the Sears Tower had a few stories to remodel. And he hadn't even known anyone hurt or killed in the attack. Yet, the sledge of emotions settling in the pit of his stomach had solidified into a cement rock weighing him down.

Sleeping in until well past 10:00 A.M., Will figured the peaceful silence resounding from his home meant his parents had done the same. They all needed some time to recuperate. Pushing off his covers, he headed downstairs to grab a bowl of cereal.

Not feeling like doing much at all, he suggested to his parents after they finally roused themselves that they all go see a movie. None of them wanted to turn on the TV and see the same destructive scenes already ingrained in their minds. And Will did not want to have to think anything about it. He had things to look forward to.

That evening the Cubs would have one of two chances left to gain the division lead over the Cardinals. With only these two games remaining in the season, both teams were tied in the standings for the National League Central Division title. Splitting the series with

Houston had not helped the situation. With Stacey coming along to the game Wednesday night, it would take a disaster to darken that season closer.

Feeling like he needed to talk after returning from the movie, he decided to call Stacey. Grabbing the phone off its base, he lay down on his unmade bed.

"Wasn't that nuts yesterday?" she asked when she first heard his voice.

"I know," replied Will. "Do you think we're going to have school tomorrow?"

"The news a little while ago said that all schools would be open," Stacey said.

"Oh, I haven't turned on the TV all day." Rolling onto his stomach, he stuffed a pillow underneath his chest.

After talking through their past two days, both seemed glad that school would give them something to do. Changing the subject to finally get to what Will really wanted to discuss, he asked, "So are you still looking forward to tomorrow night?"

"Definitely," she replied enthusiastically. "I've been thinking about it all day long."

"Same with me," he said a little too quickly, frustrating himself that he showed his feelings for her way too easily.

"My parents still aren't too thrilled with it, though. It took me almost a half hour to talk them into it," she stated matter-of-factly.

As if on cue, Will's parents came to his bedroom door. His mother rolled a finger upward in a beckoning motion. "Ah, Stacey, I gotta go. We'll talk more at school tomorrow."

"Wait. We're leaving straight from school, right?" she asked.

"Yes. Bring whatever you need with you. See ya then," he said as he clicked off the phone. A lump formed in the pit of his stomach as his parents turned and looked at each other as if trying to decide who would start.

"Will, your father and I have been talking about the game tomorrow," his mother started.

"O.K. What about it?" he responded as though asking for a reason for what he suspected was coming.

"We don't feel that it would be a safe time, after all, to go to the game tomorrow," his mother said as delicately as possible.

"I'll be with Ryan's dad," Will pointed out, not wanting to leave room for discussion.

"We know. It's not that sort of safety we're talking about," she defensively replied. "You can watch the game here. We'll make a big night out of it. You can invite Stacey if you want," she said convincingly.

"I already invited her to go *to* the game," he urged.

"I know."

"Dad, you agreed that I could go if I finished the paper."

Suddenly getting the most eerie feeling that he more than wanted to go, that he somehow needed to be there, he added, "Plus it's a once-in-a-lifetime game, and it'd do me some good to have something positive and exciting right now."

Knowing that he had used his best bargaining tool, he saw a faint resigned look trickle onto his mother's face. His father, who had remained silent until this point stated, "Maybe it would do him some good. He's really been looking forward to it. I would sure welcome the chance to do something enjoyable and not have to think about what's been going on for a while."

As if the matter had been settled, Will hurriedly hugged his mother, not giving her a chance to rescind the decision. "Come on. We can still make a big night out of tonight's game," he said as he quickly led them downstairs to the TV.

His lightened mood grew as a very patriotic display preceded the game. With the series taking place at home, Chicago obviously also intended to make a huge night out of this. With a full day to prepare, workers had decked out the stadium with red, white, and blue bunting, and famous entertainers from all around were on hand to sing the national anthem together. While fireworks blasted above their chorused voices, Will's chest expanded with the swelling of pride.

His body pulsing, he too felt for the first time that terror could not strike him down. He was part of the home of the brave and the land of the free. After discussing terrorist acts in his English class and spending so much time writing that paper for Mr. Tenepior, he felt as though he were somehow standing up against these acts on his very own. He was glad he had written about stopping terrorism. He felt connected to this day more than what he thought most other kids would.

In much the same way, the Cubs seemed to surge with the very same energy. With no outs in the bottom of the very first inning, their cleanup batter crushed a four-bagger to give the Cubs a four-run lead. Terror could not harm this. All was good with the world once again.

Will believed games like this were important. It was imperative for Chicago to once again feel whole. Will fervently felt that sports had the power to bring people together. It allowed them to enjoy themselves. It helped them feel like life was exciting, passionate, normal. Chicago's citizens would come in droves to the stadium for these games feeling tense and yet brave because they somehow knew and wanted to be a part of the unity and joy of the sport.

Will expected that infectious feeling would ignite the largest patriotic following the stadium had ever seen. He wanted to be a part of this record-breaking crowd anxious for energy and hope—a feeling that would rise above all and shout, "You can't knock us down!"

Unfortunately, there were more than just sports fans who understood this as well. There were some, in fact, who had been counting on it.

Chapter 10

Though the Cubs cruised to an easy win that night, so had the Cardinals. Waking up the next morning with his hair in disheveled heaps, Will headed immediately for the shower. Looking in the bathroom mirror, he saw his eyes had the jagged streaks of a stressful night of sleeplessness. Breathing deeply, he tried to relax. This was to be the greatest day of his life.

He and the girl of his dreams would get to spend the night watching his favorite team trying to secure a playoff berth. Having complete control over their own destiny, the Cubs had a chance to either win the title outright or at least force a division series game. Will had never before anticipated a day with so much excitement or so much on the line.

Since it was the first day back after the disaster, his classes were taking a break from the regular curriculum. Making the most of the teachable moment, many of his teachers were touching on some facet of how Monday had affected them all. Expecting much of the same in Tenepior's class, Will had come prepared with his report in hand. That's when the only really unusual thing happened.

Walking into his classroom, Will was greeted by a substitute teacher. Mr. Tenepior had never missed a day of school before. And this was the last day anyone would expect him to miss. Mr. Tenepior seemed to live for moments like this.

Left with no other option, Will took his report to the sub. "Would you please make sure Mr. Tenepior gets this?"

"Is he expecting it?" asked the sub.

"He told me to bring it in by the end of the week, Ma'm," he said.

"O.K. I'll be sure to leave it for him on his desk," she replied.

The rest of the day seemed to flash past as all Will could now think about was his night with Stacey. He had never looked forward to another night like he did this.

Arriving at Wrigley Field around 5:00 P.M., the four walked around taking in the atmosphere for a good hour. The late afternoon air was uncharacteristically warm for this time of year—perfect for leisurely looking and window shopping. Walking hand in hand to the stadium, Will and Stacey posed for pictures in front of the red Wrigley Field sign. Having a digital camera, Stacey had a little more difficult than the others entering through the gates. Added security had already made the ticket lines crowded as people waited to have every purse or tote thoroughly searched.

Becoming a little discouraged that this hassle would leave Stacey a bit disheartened about the evening, Will tried to divert her attention by taking her over to one of the numerous gear stands to buy her whatever Cubs' hat she liked the best. Secretly this was a double bonus for him because he thought the entrancing deepness of her blue eyes was enhanced even further by the blue that dominated most Cubs' merchandise.

Finding their seats underneath the green overhang on the left field side, they watched batting practice and took cool sips of their Coca-Colas. There was energy in the air. The crowd was buzzing. The players seemed to skip around the field. The balls soared off the bats as players swung. Not a seat was left in the stadium and hundreds of people were standing around the fenced guardrails.

Stacey seemed to say it best. "This is incredible."

"Hey, remind me who you guys got your tickets from," chided Ryan.

With a playful nudge, Will pushed him with his forearm.

Ryan leaned over to whisper in Will's ear, "Remember, you owe me big!"

Stacey, being too smart for her own good, overheard his little comment. She leaned over to Ryan and added, "Ryan, if you'd like to go to the movies with us on Friday, I'm sure I could talk Samantha into coming."

Apparently Stacey was also aware of the affection Ryan had held for Samantha since grade school. A grin that could not be suppressed formed across Ryan's face as his neck grew redder and redder. Realizing Stacey had already scheduled another date, Will was as elated as Ryan. Slapping a spirited high-five, they both shouted, "Score!" in unison.

As predicted, the game was electric. Although displaying a stout pitching duel, both teams nitpicked their way, working hard to earn runs. By the bottom of the fifth inning, the Astros were one run ahead.

With runners in scoring positions, the Cubs' batter swung hard, screeching a foul ball in their direction. Arcing through the air and somehow just managing to miss the overhang, the ball started dropping down right above them. As the crowd raised their hands and shifted their bodies to position themselves to grab that ball, Stacey launched herself off her seat skyward, reaching out with the hat torn from her head. Outdistancing all of them, she swung leftward, snatching the ball before any fingertips could grasp it.

Completely stunned that Stacey could out-catch a couple of club team all-star baseball players, Will and Ryan sat completely dumbfounded as she handed over the ball. Combining two of Will's favorite fixations, he realized that Stacey's catch had to be the single most exhilarating and phenomenally beautiful thing he had ever seen. He knew he had to marry this woman someday.

Kicking, clawing, and scratching their way, the Cubs managed a run off a suicide squeeze before the end of the inning.

Bringing back a couple of frozen lemonades, Ryan's father said to Stacey, "You might want to go out for the season this year. I saw you on the TV monitors downstairs. I bet you could give these boys a run for their money."

Flashing that perfect smile of hers, she replied, "Just thought I'd show Will here what kinda catch *he's* made."

"I can tell you'll definitely keep him on his toes," Ryan's father said, squeezing out a few chuckles.

Asking Will to hang on to the ball for her, Stacey settled into her seat again and they all slurped up their slightly melted freezes. Ryan wiped a drop of juice off his lips with his shirt sleeve. Shaking his head, Ryan told Stacey, "After seeing your moves with that catch, I'm definitely going to need a pair of those Treks now."

Treks. A tsunami of images reverberated through Will's thoughts. Individual frames of color and light floated before his eyes like encryptions from an Enigma machine. Taking shape, the rounded corners of splicings melded into odd factions of puzzle pieces skewing and rolling into a fitted silhouette. A thunderous pounding pulsated his jugular with the increased pressure exploding in his brain. It was his short story unit, rosin bag throw, and English essay tests all over again.

"No way!" Will rocketed out of his seat, spilling a slushy mess all over his right shoe. At his sudden move, they all glanced at him with total bewilderment. But the images of a bombing bewildered him the most. For a second all he could manage to mutter aloud was, "No way!"

"Will, what is it?" Stacey questioned.

With a distant look in his eyes, Will fixed his eyes on the green scoreboard in center field. He worried about the notion nagging at his consciousness—not wanting to trust its possibility but fearing its absolute reality.

"Will?" The worry was apparent in the slow quaver of Stacey's voice.

Unblinking, Will turned and looked down at Stacey, boring his intense stare deep into her eyes. She seemed so pure and good, so real and true as she inquisitively looked back up at him—such a stark contrast to the mere whim infiltrating his thoughts. Redirecting his eyes back to the individual squares of the manual scoreboard, seemingly so unspoiled in their historical simplicity that Will couldn't help but consider that he would very simply sound like a fool if he told her his thoughts.

Shaking his head as if he had just been confused, he said, "Ah, nothing. I, I just thought I saw somebody I knew." But he knew Ryan wouldn't think he was crazy. Hoping his flushed heated cheeks would come off as embarrassment, he added, "Ryan, come with me to get some napkins so I can clean off this mess." Not allowing him a chance to decline, Will pulled him up by his arm.

Forced into submission, Ryan uttered "O.K. Alright."

After stepping over legs into the free space of the stairway, Ryan turned to Will who was now suddenly sweating profusely. "What in the heck was that all about?"

Again grabbing his arm, Will pulled Ryan like a dog on a leash. Trying to find a spot with few people around, Will stopped pulling Ryan when they reached the rear cement walking ramp. Stopping to get his breath by grasping his fingers through the green wired screen, he decided it was safe to speak.

"O.K. You're never going to believe this. I'm not sure I believe it myself." He paused, swallowed deeply and glanced about all around him. "Remember the other night when we all got together to watch the game at your place?"

"Yeah," Ryan replied suspiciously.

"There was that Treks commercial you were so interested in," he stammered. A nervous anxiousness was apparent in his voice.

"O.K."

"And remember the report that I had to write for Tenepior?"

"What's all that got to do with spilling lemonade all over yourself?" Ryan asked with agitation.

"Where did that commercial take place?" Will asked trying to put all the pieces together.

"The runner jogged over the Sears Tower." Ryan's voice was shaky with confusion.

"Exactly."

"So?"

"Think about my report!"

Ryan, only grasping half of the situation, muttered sarcastically, "Are you trying to say that the commercial has something to do with the bombing?"

Continuing to talk through his thoughts while ignoring Ryan's skepticism, Will ventured, "I think the terrorists who bombed the Sears Tower were signaled by that commercial to plan the attack. Remember how he gave a thumbs-up sign? I think it was a green light to go ahead with the attack."

Ryan slowly nodded his recognition of where Will was headed. "I know you're usually two steps ahead of everyone else on things like this, but..."

"It was right in front of that parking lane," Will cut in, not letting Ryan finish his comment.

"That's right. I remember there was a bus parked there when that runner landed back on the ground," Ryan said excitedly. Will had not thought about that.

"That could have been signaling that they were to use a bus for the bomb," Will pieced together.

"That's way too much of a coincidence. So what do we have now, marathon runners who bomb large buildings?" Ryan asked.

"That's right!" Will shouted, now drawing a little attention from a couple of spectators coming up the ramp behind them. Trying to whisper now, he said, "The marathon runner's jersey number was #101. That's the date! That's what day it happened. Monday was October 1st!"

"Man, how do you remember stuff like that?"

Not wanting to waste the time recounting the most sacred event of his life when he first held hands with Stacey, he shrugged it off. There was no way he was forgetting anything about that moment.

Ryan shifted from foot to foot. As he raised his head to look at Will, he suggested, "It happened at 9:00 A.M., right? The shoe price on the ad was $90. I bet that was a signal too." As the pieces started to fit together, Ryan added, "I bet everything in that ad was a clue."

Ryan's affirmation of his theory made Will panic even more. If they were right, they were in a big fix. Alarmed, Will's breath grew short. "But Ryan, think about the other commercial!" Will urged with a horrified insistence.

"That's right! Sunday night at my house." Ryan chortled, "I didn't think you were paying attention to anything but talking to Stacey on the phone."

"We saw it before I called her. Now, come on. What was it about?" Will urgently pleaded.

"That's right. Well, it was about that streaker running around Wrigley Field." Ryan turned to point out at the field marking where the streaker had run when he suddenly whipped back around, his eyes wide open. "There's going to be another attack!"

"Here! At Wrigley Field!" Will stated matter-of-factly to catch Ryan up. "We gotta think back through that commercial!"

"He held the thumbs-up out on the street under that grey stone building with the bleachers. I bet that's where they'll put a bomb."

"That's what I was thinking."

"But when?" asked Ryan. As if copying Will's head shift, Ryan looked at that leftfield foul pole and said, "Those flags are the numbers of Ernie Banks, Ron Santo, and Ferguson Jenkins. Ron Santo's number was 10."

"October. Right." Suddenly Will jerked upright again and craned his neck to see the game. "Oh, no!"

"What? What?" Ryan questioned. The worry seeped from his tone.

"What inning is it?" he quickly wanted to know.

"Bottom of the sixth. Why?" Ryan asked. "Tonight! It's going to be tonight!" screeched Ryan as he answered himself. "The streaker slid down the scoreboard. It said that the Cubs had three runs."

"We've got to do something," Will said pointedly, already chewing over a plan. "October 3rd can't become another 9/11. Get your dad and Stacey out of here quickly. I'll go for help."

Wanting to make sure the people in the stadium he cared for most were free from danger, he knew it would be left up to him to try and stop this alone.

Chapter 11

Weaving his way through blue clad spectators, Will raced out of the stadium. He couldn't help but think that all of this was not happening. This couldn't be. It was too far-fetched. With all the added police and other security in the city, the terrorists had to be either nuts or desperate to try it a second time so close to the last strike. Surely with all those police, they would be caught.

Then Will turned these thoughts in his mind as he sorted fact from fiction. These were terrorists. One had to be nuts and desperate to do this kind of thing. Mr. Tenepior had said in a classroom discussion once, *"A desperate person does not act in a rational way."*

They had been discussing *Fahrenheit 451* by Ray Bradbury, where a woman throws her own body onto a pile of her own burning books and goes up in flames along with them. This lesson made Will wonder what kind of life Mr. Tenepior lived to want to teach these types of things to his students. It seemed like an odd lesson at the time for a bunch of eighth graders. But now it had become useful.

Still sorting through his thoughts, he mused that an irrational person would not be concerned with the added security. Actually, no one in his or her right mind would expect a second attack now.

"That's exactly why they are going to do it! They'll get away with it because no one will see it coming," shouted Will to himself as he rounded the corner toward Sheffield Avenue.

It was this very thought that kept Will from immediately grabbing some police officer. The seventh inning had already started. It would take too long to explain it all to an incredulous adult. And who would believe a kid anyway? Feeling the pressure of time, he had to act quickly.

Sprinting across the street, he slammed his body against the door of the apartment building reading "3621 Sheffield." Needing to search quickly, he ran up each set of stairways. Not finding anything looking suspicious, he suddenly realized it wouldn't be in the grey stone building. The terrorists had already made the mistake of being too far away from their target. They had to get it closer.

Running back out to the street, he scanned the entire area. He would have searched each t-shirt stand on the block, but they all were set up across the street from the stadium. Facing the street, he tried to think. He cursed himself for not seeing it earlier. There had been a U-Haul parked by the curb in that commercial. As if Tenepior were standing there himself, Will once again heard his teacher's voice ring out in his mind. *"Always support your thoughts with evidence from the text."* Reading the commercial like a book, he decided he had to be right. No sensible person would try moving into one of these apartments during game time.

Looking both directions, he didn't see a U-Haul anywhere around and wondered just how in the world he would stop a truck.

Just then, booming from the stadium came a loudspeaker voice, "Alright, Cub fans. With a one. A two. A three."

As if attached to a stopwatch, the engine of an orange colored U-Haul truck heading straight in his direction roared two blocks away. He had to act now.

Sprinting over to the red bricked corner where several policemen were standing, Will knew that he had made a mistake not getting their attention before. Grabbing a green wooden sawhorse normally used to direct the hoards of walking baseball fans, he pulled it out to block the street. The cops, suddenly noticing that a kid had taken off with their barrier, started running forward yelling, "Halt!"

The truck, approaching the wooden barrier, accelerated with a thunderous rev of its engines. Police whistles blared to Will's right. Closing fast only several hundred feet away, the driver of the U-Haul either didn't see Will or intended to run right through him.

"Will, watch out!" screamed a higher-pitched voice he heard above all others. Swiveling his head, he saw Stacey running out ahead of both Ryan and his father. Her head was turned toward the speeding truck now only seconds away from Will's body.

The cops reached Will first and grabbed his arms. Shouting at the top of his lungs and trying to point, Will screamed, "Truck!"

One policeman let go of his arm and looked up. Straightening himself and lifting his arms out in the air as if bracing himself for impact, he yelled in the truck's direction, "Stop!" The other cop reacted by raising his short-handled stop sign.

Will could see the truck was not slowing down. Panicked, he was jolted by a momentary regret and stole a last uncertain glance over his right shoulder at Stacey. For the first time realizing that she was in harm's way, he felt a stronger-than-ever need to do something, anything, to stop it.

Reaching into his pocket, he found Stacey's foul ball. Sliding two fingers around the threads, he gripped it hard. Diving out of the way, the police officers jumped to safety across the pavement. While diving, one grabbed for Will. Stumbling a little, Will still managed to plant his feet firmly. Feeling like this might be his only chance, he threw a left elbow downward to deflect the outstretched arms of the officer. In the same motion, he heaved his arm forward and released the ball, sending it sailing directly at the U-Haul's windshield with only a half-second to spare. With a crack, the glass shattered into a cobweb of crooked angles. The force of the throw sent Will hurling to his left as he fell to his knee.

Screeching tires bellowed from the pavement as the vehicle swerved rightward and slammed into the very right edge of the sawhorse, splintering the wooden 2X4 as it crashed against the curb. Missing Will by inches, the vehicle did not stop. As if in slow motion, the driver rotated his head sideways and focused his menacing gaze directly on Will's face. Though only for a split second, the driver locked his disbelieving eyes on the face of a kid. And in the same instant, the U-Haul gunned past the stadium and on down Sheffield Avenue. Will could hear the squealing tires as the truck rounded a corner blocks down the road.

Reaching his side, Stacy practically threw her body on top of him and grabbed at his face to see if he had been hurt. "Will?" she cried.

Through sweat-stained eyes, he smiled back at her. As he tried to reply, he was gruffly jerked into the air.

"What's the meaning of all this?" roared an extremely angry policeman.

Still holding onto his wits, Will knew the officers would never buy his explanation. He innocently said, "I saw that truck speeding out of control, and I didn't want anyone to get hurt."

Off to his left he could hear the mechanical voice of the other officer speaking on his radio, calling a search for U-Hauls in the area.

Sliding next to him were Ryan and his father. Both were panting wildly. Ryan's eyes were as big as melons. "That was incredible!" he shouted gleefully toward Will as a handful of other officers joined the scene.

The officer was not done with him. "You about got yourself killed," he said as he shook Will a little.

"Blame that on the driver," Will choked out, realizing that he had unwisely snapped at the officer.

Looking over at Ryan's dad, the officer grunted, "This your son?"

Mr. Moritz bent over, holding his hands on his knees to try to control his breathing. "No. But he's under my supervision tonight."

"Some supervision," replied the cop disdainfully as he shook his head. Glancing around and digging into his breast pocket for a notepad, he grumbled, "I don't see that any violations have necessarily been broken unless the driver of that U-Haul reports the shattered windshield. I'll simply need to take down each of your names for my files."

Flipping his notepad over to finalize his notes, the officer glared at Ryan's father while Ryan skipped around behind him buzzing with excited energy. Tilting his head so one eye peered directly at Mr. Moritz, the officer stated, "With an arm like that maybe he should spend more time in the stadium than out here on the street."

Mr. Moritz placed his hand under Will's elbow and pulled him away. "I'm taking that as permission to leave." Stacey, still at his side, rested her head on his shoulder as they walked and tightly held onto his hand with both of hers.

Shuffling backwards facing Will and Stacey, Ryan was still shaking his head. "Man that was so cool! I can't wait to tell everyone about it."

After they had walked a short distance, Ryan's dad finally stopped. He pulled everyone off to the side against the stadium wall and flashed Will a baffled glare. "Now explain what that was all about. Ryan found us and told us we had to leave immediately—that you needed help. We hardly had a second to blink and he took off running."

"That's when we saw you standing in the way of that truck," interjected Stacey.

"Now I want to know what's up and how you two are involved," Ryan's father demanded.

As Ryan and Will began their story, both Stacey and Mr. Moritz stood with blank disbelieving stares. Starting with seeing the commercials, they each told their accounts of what had happened. As they explained the clues they had pieced together, Will felt his face swell with redness and heat. The smile adorning Stacey's lips moments before had flat-lined, tightening together to show her agitation. Noting Stacey's crossed arms, he could feel her skepticism. Listening to Ryan explain how it boiled down to shoe commercials, Will couldn't help but hear the absurdity in what they were saying.

It sound like one of their cops-and-robber stories they used to make up as kids. Gathering the same look from Ryan's dad as they had back when they were small, Will could see how far-out this all really seemed. He felt like he was climbing a rock face without any footholds within reach.

"I don't believe it," Mr. Moritz muttered disgustedly. "If it were true, why didn't you tell me or run to get help?" His pause forced Will to swallow hard. Mr. Motitz continued, "Your two imaginations have gotten the best of you, and they almost got you killed. How would I have explained that to your parents? Commercials, ha! Just tell me one thing then. Why didn't your 'U-Haul terrorist' just run his truck into the stadium and blow it up? He was right there. I don't think one little broken windshield would stop a suicide bomber."

For that, Will did not have an answer.

Will agreed, "You're right, Mr. Moritz. There's no possible way that commercial had anything to do with planning these attacks."

"What?" Ryan sputtered.

"Think about it. There have to be thousands of ways to communicate their plans. They wouldn't just stick it out there on TV for everyone to see, let alone during a nationally broadcasted game. It was probably just a coincidence that a U-Haul had been in the commercial."

Stacey interjected, "And there are always busses in that lane at the Sears Tower. One was probably just there when they shot the commercial." Throwing her arms into the air and rolling her eyes, she turned a few steps away, staring back at the stadium. Will could read her well enough to know he had wrecked what would have been a wonderful evening chasing that fool-hearted notion.

"Yeah, that's probably true. Everything would be traced back to the Treks shoe company, anyway. They'd be busted for sure." Staring at the sticky stain left on his shoe, Will concluded with, "I'm sorry, Mr. Moritz, for having been so much trouble tonight."

"But," Ryan faltered. "But that still doesn't explain the fact that a U-Haul just tried running you over."

"Look at this street. It's filled with tons of apartments. There's probably a U-Haul going through here every day," Mr. Moritz explained.

With a disgusted humph, "Probably some drunk driver," completed Stacey from over her shoulder.

Will, feeling completely embarrassed at how ridiculous the whole story sounded, finally said, "Stacey, I hope you don't think I'm going nuts."

Turning back around, Stacey's fist pounded downward with the trilling of her voice as she fumed, "You had to go and throw away this evening just like you threw away my baseball. Did you even consider how all that would make me feel?"

Overhead fireworks started blazing in the now-darkening sky signaling a Cubs' win. Everyone but the two of them looked up. People began running out of the bars onto the streets screaming at the top of their lungs. Each flaring explosion accented Stacey's tightened lips and drilling eyes.

As if finally accepting Will's debacle, Ryan added salt to the wound, "You mean, you mean none of this was actually true? And now we missed the biggest game of our lives?"

"I guess that's what we get for allowing you guys to watch so much TV," Mr. Moritz concluded.

Ryan shook his head from side to side and started walking off down the street in the direction of where they had parked several blocks away. "I'm sorry," Will called ahead, hoping that Ryan would forgive him for missing the game.

"Let's get home. Maybe we can catch some highlights. There's been way too much excitement here for one night," sighed Mr. Moritz. In single file, they all shuffled off toward the car, oblivious to the exuberance of the people on the street.

Noticing the vacancy of his still cupped hand, Will paused, glancing back over his shoulder to the asphalt where moments before he had nearly been crushed beneath the speeding tires. Inadvertently fingering the seamed mesh of his Cubs' jersey for the grooves of tread he thought should be there, a shudder of realization riveted his body. He had almost been killed. And though he still breathed, he had caused Stacey to feel deflated. And why? Because he had come to believe in an idiotic notion planted there by an overly demanding teacher who had meant to punish him. "Freaking Mr. Tenepior," he fumed angrily. If only Mr. Tenepior weren't so idealistic. If only he himself hadn't acted so irrationally. If only it had all been true, Stacey would see him as a hero.

If only Will had given it some more thought, he might have realized something very important; something so important men in search of it had risked their lives. Will would have realized he had seen the face of the U-Haul's driver. The face of a man on a horrifying mission. A face that alone could strike terror.

Chapter 12

Will attempted to make amends with Ryan the next day in the hallway, but every time he got close, Ryan would slam his locker and storm away. He tried but had much the same result with Stacey. He contemplated that maybe he should try asking Samantha if she would go out with Ryan. That might bring him around, but then again, Stacey had probably already told her how immature she thought both Ryan and he were. He considered maybe trying something in Tenepior's class since they all had eighth hour together, but he was still mad at Mr. Tenepior. Wanting to have someone else to blame, he might as well blame a teacher.

After his surprising absence, Mr. Tenepior was back and ready to discuss Monday's events. Not wanting to think any more about it, Will remained as quiet as he could. Not waiting to be called on, Ryan announced, "Will has a new theory that he didn't write about in his report."

Turning around to catch the smile smeared across Ryan's face, Will sank lower into his chair. He suspected that this was Ryan's attempt to pay him back for missing part of last night's game. Not desiring his blunder to be brought up, especially in front of Stacey, he let out a frustrated huff. The last thing he wanted was for her to dwell on his idiotic stupidity of the night before.

"So Will. What might that be?" asked an interested Mr. Tenepior.

"Nothing," he said untruthfully.

"Come on. Tell him how you think terrorists make shoe commercials," Ryan pushed amongst a raucous laughter coming from those students who had already heard about it.

Now giving his full attention, Mr. Tenepior shifted his body to directly face Will. "What's all this, Will?" Tenepior's question stifled the chuckles.

This question had not been the usual challenge; Will could feel the earnestness of the inquiry. He could also feel the potential energy of his fellow students coiled like a spring. As if taking their cue from Stacy's refusal to even look up from her desk, students sat rigidly as silence charged the air. They seemed eager to get the rare chance to see the entertainment of a dating conflict play out in the classroom if Will spilled his guts.

Will knew this probably wouldn't go well, but he figured it might give him the chance to explain himself. Almost apologetically, he began to speak. Rather than replying to Mr. Tenepior, he shifted and directed his voice toward Stacey. Will summarized his seeing the commercials and putting it all together at the ball field. "I thought it was a perfect idea for the terrorists to want to strike right then. Everyone in the city was already tense, but no one would have guessed that a second attack would occur with all the added police on the streets."

Shaking his head in disbelief as to how preposterous this all sounded now, he tried to explain through his bumbling, "It all seemed to fit at the time. I mean look at the cities that have had terrorist attacks: San Francisco, St. Louis, Boston. They all have major league teams. New York has two. If terrorists just tuned to their locally televised games, they would get the message. Treks are sports shoes, and I've only seen the commercials during game broadcasts."

"That's a very interesting theory, Will," interjected Mr. Tenepior.

With a rise of anger, Ryan sneered, "Tell him how you single-handedly took on the terrorist attack of a U-Haul." A rise of laughter kinetically flooded through the rows of students as if an over-saturated water balloon had been tossed and found its mark.

Will pushed to see any change in Stacey's demeanor. He was obviously hurting her to go through it all over again as he watched her reddened eyes staring straight forward.

Mr. Tenepior looked up from his scribbled note-taking. The waves of student activity turned to small ripples.

Making it sound like less of an adventure than it really had been, Will quickly told how he had altered the driving path of the truck. "At first I thought it was all true." Pleading with his voice, he tried sounding as convincing as he could. "It would have possibly canceled the playoffs of America's pastime. When I considered this, I thought about how most sporting events weren't halted after 9/11. And why? Because they help us to feel normal and make us excited to live. That's what I thought the terrorists were after. A way to make us lose hope," he concluded with a double entendre as he pressed Stacey to feel what he was trying to say.

Budding at the corner of her eye was a single tear. As it spilled over the roundness of her cheek, she turned and looked straight into his eyes. His hopefulness was crunched by the regret that now clenched his teeth.

Breaking the tender moment, Mr. Tenepior said, "That's the best case building I've seen all year!"

"But," Will turned and watched as Ryan's expressions changed from a dropped jaw to squinting eyes, surely contemplating a way to come out ahead on this. Then suddenly raising his eyebrows, Ryan blurted out, "And I thought the price of the shoes was telling what time to detonate the bomb. Like $90 meant 9:00." Though Will was sure Ryan thought he had just scored a point for himself, for some reason a few students found this vaguely funny.

Mr. Tenepior said, "Maybe, but let's be realistic today and figure out why all of this cannot be true."

Ryan slammed his spiral notebook to his desk. Will heard him mutter under his breath, "I can't catch a break."

Although being charred by his gut instinct just the night before, Will couldn't help but surmise that Mr. Tenepior was evading the issue. It was completely uncharacteristic of him to tear down an idea that seemed like original thinking.

"First of all," Mr. Tenepior started, holding one finger up in the air, "let's examine the number on the athlete's jersey. #101 could also mean January first. How would noncommunicating terrorists be able to tell which date to plan for? Secondly, there's a whole problem dealing with the fact that there was no bombing at Wrigley Field last night. I heard your story about the U-Haul, but there are probably hundreds of explanations for that. Without a second bombing, there is absolutely no credibility to your theory."

Several heads turned toward Will. He knew it was Tenepior's fault that he had even come up with any of these ideas in the first place.

Why had every single thought of his been critiqued with a magnifying glass? What had it all been for then? What was the point of coming up with original thoughts if Tenepior was just going to make fun of them? Mr. Tenepior's credibility was what had been crushed in his eyes. No longer would he push himself like he had. No longer would he participate. He was finished.

"Oh, and one other thing. I heard on the news this morning that some U-Haul had sideswiped several vehicles before being pulled over. The driver had been arrested for DUI, but there was nothing about a bomb. Sorry, Will, but nice try."

With several chuckles, the class rose out of their seats as the bell rang for the day—a day that had been humiliating for Will. Now only caring about what Stacey thought and hardly even paying attention to what Mr. Tenepior had just said, Will sat there hoping Stacey would walk by his desk on her way out. She didn't. She rose and, without looking at him, walked around the rows of desks before heading out the classroom door.

Rising to leave his seat and not spend a moment more of this frustrating day at school, he turned to trudge out of the room.

"Will, stop. I need to speak to you for a moment," called Mr. Tenepior.

Glancing over his shoulder as he contemplated whether to continue walking or not, Will stopped, remembering what had happened the last time he hadn't followed Tenepior's directions. Deciding he didn't want to be assigned another report, he walked over to the teacher's desk.

Still staring hard at Will, Mr. Tenepior finally spoke. "Will, I want you to do something for me."

Not holding back, Will replied, "I think I've already done enough for you." Deciding that in fact this all had been a waste of his time, he turned to leave the room as he tried to forget anything and everything Tenepior had ever taught him.

With reluctance in his voice, Mr. Tenepior muttered, "Will."

Waving him off with the flick of his wrist, Will rounded the corner desk.

"Will."

Nearing the door, Will reached for the knob.

Mr. Tenepior whispered, "I believe every word you said."

Almost stumbling with his next step, Will thought about pausing for a second, but anger drove him forward to the door.

Heaving an exhausted sigh, Mr. Tenepior called out to Will's departing back, "In fact, I more than believe you. Truthfully, I think you may have solved the whole mystery."

Chapter 13

Halting midway through the door, Will swung himself around. Was Tenepior playing some sort of game? "What?"

"I think you heard me," replied Mr. Tenepior shortly.

"You believed the whole story?" he asked in disbelief peppered with a little caution that Tenepior might also be setting him up again.

"In fact, I think it may be exactly the breakthrough I have been searching for," he said, baffling Will.

"But you yourself pointed out several holes in my theory." Will stared at him as if this whole conversation was even more ludicrous than his own presumptions had been. "Like the bombless U-Haul you said the cops pulled over? That's got to be proof that none of this was ever actually true."

"For the rest of the students' sake, I made that up. They needed to hear it."

Will's mind reeled. This undoubtedly had to be the most confusing conversation he had ever had. Why would Tenepior have lied to the class? And if this were true, then why had Tenepior made a mockery of his ideas? If he could distort the truth in this situation, what else might he have lied about?

"Why? Then why in the world did you say all those things about it not possibly being true in front of the whole class?" he asked through clenched teeth.

"If you would think for a second, I bet you could figure that out for yourself," Mr. Tenepior said, indicating his student should still do the thinking for himself.

"Forget it! I don't care about your explanation. It'll probably be another lie anyway." Never having spoken to a teacher or an adult in this way before, Will twitched with nervousness, sure that his trust in Mr. Tenepior had been wasted.

With nothing else to lose, Will's confidence blossomed with the anger that enveloped him. He had faced a speeding truck trying to run him down. He could stand up to this pathetic excuse for a teacher. Hands shaking, he slammed the textbook still in his hands to the floor and stomped away from his desk. "I'm done! You're lying. You ruined the best night of my life. And now all my friends think I'm psychotic."

"Will, for one second, ask yourself what would happen if there were thirty teenagers who all knew of a secret terrorist operation?"

"Who cares?" Will screeched, his voice too high and tensed with emotion. Shoving desks out of his way and kicking at one that snagged his backpack, he headed to the door.

"I bet those people at the game last night would."

That stopped him. Was Tenepior saying that he might actually have saved all of their lives? Did he truly believe his story?

Trying to understand, Will turned back to face him. "You think my classmates would all go running out and try to stop a situation like I did last night." Amending his statement as he continued to slowly process the thought, "And you don't want to feel like you would be the cause of it all if something happened to any of them."

"Good! I'm glad to see you've learned a little of what I tried teaching you this year. Rule number one when gathering information is to always try and see things from others' point-of-view." He paused and quickly added, "Remember that!"

With that simple order, Will felt partially defeated at how quickly Mr. Tenepior had regained control of their heated exchange. He still wasn't sure, though, that he wasn't being messed with.

As if reading Will's mind, Mr. Tenepior asked, "If you don't believe me, then consider what teenagers do that could possibly damage any hopes of catching these guys?"

While Will and Mr. Tenepior spoke, unbeknownst to them, outside the school building waited a man. A man with a debt to be paid. Poised on a knobby little hill hidden by a small pine tree, he watched each student come screaming and laughing out of the front doors of the school. Shoving the doors widely, swells of kids noisily bounced out. The man's fiery, intense eyes locked fanatically onto the face of each student passing beneath the squared steel frames. He silently calculated the look and appearance of each as his finger twitched distinctly at every similarity. Purging though the array of facial characteristics, he scanned each face, probing for the combination hardened in his mind.

Between the branches, propped up in front of his positioned body, set the blackened metal surface of a high-powered rifle. Delicately twisted into the barrel's tip, was the cylinder shape of a silencer—a silencer put in place not only to smother sound, but also to silence the life of one particular teenage boy. He had risked everything by making a journey to police headquarters to search for the teenager's name that would have appeared on a report filed the night before. This same report detailed proof of his own blunder—a blunder that should have been his finest hour, but was stopped by a menacing kid who had to pay the price for stepping in his way.

Peering though his scope, he pinpointed each face with his crosshairs. Raging pulses of hate surged through his arms all the way to his fingertip. Arching over the trigger, his finger played "duck, duck, goose" picking which of the fellow students he would shoot along with Will Conlan. He had to make this look like a random shooting. He did not want it traced back to the incident of the night before.

Patiently waiting to find the young man he longed to see crumpling over in death, he couldn't help but tense at the prospect of not seeing him leave the school. He had positioned himself facing the direction the main doors opened toward, but he could also see two other exits. Only a few students had trickled out those doors. None had been the one he wanted to find.

Slowly the stream of students dwindled as he faced the probability that his boy was being detained inside. With this new certainty, he knew that no longer could he make this out to be a random attack. Deciding now to abduct the teen, he would end his miserable life and hide his body where it would never be found.

Stealthily taking apart his gun and packing it into a shoulder strapped case, he readied himself for a quick attack. Stashing his gear in the vehicle parked behind him, he grabbed a rag and some twine. Wanting to be prepared to quickly subdue Will, he looked over his supplies to find anything else he would need. Loosening the lethal blade of his knife from his waist belt, he gripped it tightly and crossed over to the schoolyard to be closer to his victim. Reaching the school's bricked wall, he flattened his body tightly against it, holding his breath with tension.

In Mr. Tenepior's classroom, the question about what teenagers do that could ruin everything still puzzled Will. "Not sure."

"Especially consider that best friend of yours."

"We blab!" he exclaimed as if belting out a quiz answer in class. "You're afraid Ryan would tell his mother and she would certainly do a news story about it."

Mr. Tenepior, who seemed three steps ahead, suddenly blurted, "There may not be much time left."

Will gave him a puzzled look at this.

"You said that you went to the game with Ryan's dad last night?" It was more of a statement than a question.

This time Will broke in, "I don't think Ryan's dad would have told his wife anything about it." With a chuckle he continued, "She might never let him go to another game if she found out. Plus I know that Mr. Moritz didn't believe a word of it himself."

Hurriedly packing up his things, Mr. Tenepior argued, "There's a good chance that Mrs. Moritz will find out about this one way or another. Heck, any one of your classmates might go home and tell his parents about what you did and word would surely reach her. Journalists never dodge a good story. We can't risk the headlines or miss this chance to catch the terrorists." Mr. Tenepior spoke all this in one breath as he dug through his suit jacket for his cell phone. Motioning Will to follow, he continued, "Walk with me. We can talk outside on the way to my car."

Chapter 14

While walking down the hallway to the door, Will and Mr. Tenepior quietly continued discussing the commercials' plots and the likelihood that anyone else knew about them.

"Will, you have made me proud to be a teacher. Not just today, but all year long," said Mr. Tenepior as they exited the door to the west of the building and walked to the teacher's rear parking lot. Mr. Tenepior pointed to his Nissan Maxima in the first stall of the lot. "I'm right here."

Walking over to the silver-colored car with him, Will paused and hesitantly asked, "I don't mean to sound unappreciative, and, if you don't mind me asking, then why have you been so hard on me this year?"

Just then, Will spotted movement out of the corner of his eye. Breaking the tension created by the question, Will turned quickly, his head snapping to the south corner of the school. Catching a glimpse of a leg darting behind the brick wall, he couldn't help but think that the person hadn't wanted to be seen. It was probably one of the guys waiting to tease him about what had happened in class.

Noticing his jerky movement, Mr. Tenepior said, "What's wrong?"

"Nothing. Someone just ran around the corner of the building."

"All this has you pretty spooked out, I would guess," Mr. Tenepior said. Will shook his head in agreement. Mr. Tenepior turned, opened his door, and sat down in the seat. Looking up at Will's puzzled look, he said, "Will?"

"Yes?"

"I'm not sure I understand your question. I call on you every class period. I always ask for your opinion on every subject. Why do you think I've been hard on you?"

"My papers seem to get more comments than any of my other classmates. And in class it seems like I get pushed harder than most everyone else."

"Will, I admit that I push you. I push all of my students. It's for your own good."

"No. It feels like most of it is directed toward me."

"That conversation is not one I have time for right now. But I will tell you this. You show potential. I wouldn't be your teacher if I didn't equip you with the skills you need to reach it. You've got a good head on your shoulders. Just make sure you use it," he said and closed the door.

He started the engine and put the car in reverse. Will could see that he had already dialed his cell phone. Rolling down the window, he signaled Will with a rolling wave of his other hand as he pulled up alongside him. Sticking out a piece of paper in his direction, Mr. Tenepior said, "I want to give you a phone number you can reach me tonight in case you remember something else that you could tell me. Also, I wouldn't be saying any of this to anyone if I were you."

"Mr. Tenepior? What are you going to do?"

"Whatever I can. You can count on that. Keep your eyes open and stay out of trouble tonight. Got it?" he said with a grin. With that, he drove away.

Deciding that he needed time to sort out all of this in his mind, Will tightened the straps on his backpack and started walking south toward home. He couldn't understand how Tenepior didn't see how he picked on him. It was so obvious to everyone else in the class. Even Kyle always made a point of making fun of him for it. Stepping off the pavement and over the curb, his shoes sank curved divots into the sodded grass. Slowly walking forward, he wanted to know the difference between pushing and picking on a person. And when did getting pushed this hard become good for someone?

As he hiked to the edge of the school building, he suddenly remembered what he had seen and tried stopping himself. At that very moment, like a blinding streak of lightning, came a fist exploding toward his jaw. If he hadn't tried to slow himself, the fist would have caught him squarely. Although he had been hammered straight to the ground, he had merely received half a blow. Luckily, the fist had glanced off his cheekbone, and he hadn't been knocked unconscious. Flashing before his eyes, a shiny razor-sharp metal blade came thrusting down at him. Swinging his right forearm sideways, Will blocked the man's wrist. In the same motion, he kicked upward with his left foot and sent his shoe sinking into his attacker's right temple.

Growling with noticeable anger, the man jumped forward, swinging the knife crazily. Will could only spin away as he dodged near life-ending slices.

Rolling to his left and grabbing at one of his fallen textbooks, Will lashed out at his attacker, slamming the corner of his book into the man's gut. At the same moment, the man stabbed the blade downward. The impact of the book shortened the man's swing a few inches, but the blade still found its target, tearing a gap into Will's side. Will instantly felt the pain. Thrusting his hands down to clamp the wound left him defenseless.

The man shot out with his boot, catching Will squarely where his hands now grasped, tearing his gut further. He curled himself to protect the injured side.

With a strong bronze-colored hand, the man clamped down on Will's jaw and stuffed a foul-smelling rag into his mouth. Lifting him off the ground with the same hand, Will squealed with agony. Pulling his now rigid, rolled-up body over to the car, the man shoved Will into the front seat.

Driving away with his knee on the wheel and tying Will up with his hands, the man grunted through a slit in his face, "You messed with the wrong person."

Driving straight for a few blocks, Will could feel the car take a corner sharply enough to squeal the tires. Will's had little doubt that this was the same man who had driven the U-Haul. Slumping himself sideways, he glanced at his captor. The right side of the man's face had a glassy appearance that reminded Will of the shattered windshield. He looked at the hairless cracking cheek and shriveled streaks running down his neck. It was the scariest face he had ever seen. Never in his worst nightmares would he have wanted to be kidnapped. And never would it have been by a man looking like death itself.

The man seemed to be studying Will too. Locking his eyes in hard, he said to Will, "Yes, you're the one. You're the kid who got in my way last night."

Still gagging on the cloth stuffed down his throat, Will tried to work it free using his tongue. Not being able to budge it at all, he tried to yell out to his captor. Hoping he would remove the gag, Will gestured with the nodding of his head.

Looking over at Will, the man spoke through the crack of his mouth, "If you yell out, it will be the last thing you ever say." Taking the end of the rag, he ripped it clear of his lips.

Breathing hard with large gasps, Will spit out, "Look. I'm sorry I threw the baseball. I thought you were going to hit me."

Squinting his eyes, he spat, "Yes, let's talk about that. What were you doing in the street during a ballgame?" the man choked out. Reaching up with his sleeve, he wiped a drip of blood from his cheek on his arm.

Secretly Will was proud inside that he had at least made this man bleed as well.

Will thought quickly. "I was waiting for a homerun ball."

"Wanted a ball, huh?" he slowly slurred. "Wanting. Always wanting. Americans never content with what they have. If they don't have it, they just go and take it no matter whose it is. Can't leave anyone alone. Always having to get what they want."

Now ranting wildly, he continued, "Making up lies so they can attack. Power hungry. America wants to rule the world and control what everyone else thinks and does and has."

Clearly enraged, the man slammed his fists against the wheel. Then, sending a spray of blood and spit against the dashboard, he shouted, "I don't believe you!" The suddenness sent shivers through Will's body.

Shuddering, Will wondered if the man thought he knew more. Contemplating telling the truth, he remembered what Mr. Tenepior had said about trying to see a situation through another person's eyes. Will didn't think there was any way this man could know that he had figured out their commercials. If he told the truth, there was no telling what he would do to him.

"Why'd you have a baseball in your pocket then? You weren't waiting for one, were you?" accused the man.

Will shot back, trying to sound confident and truthful. "Most everyone on the street carries a ball. If the opposing team hits a homerun, they keep that ball and throw the one they had in their pocket back into the stadium. The fans in the bleachers will start calling for it if the ball doesn't come back. It's a Cubs' tradition."

Glancing a searching eye back at him, the man pondered the possible truth of this statement. Will, seeing the contemplation in his eye, tried to send the lie home by saying, "No one would throw back any ball hit out of the park in a game like that."

"Maybe that is the truth. But it doesn't matter anyway. You have seen me and I can't have that. Seeing me will be the last thing you ever do." He then pulled the vehicle over very suddenly into a grove of trees. As if punctuating his last statement, the man wove the vehicle around tree after tree, giving Will the impression from their remote location that he was most definitely in for it. Scale-like Juniper shoots scraped against the car's windows before it lurched forward with a stop.

Getting out, the man came over to Will's side and pulled him to the grass with a tug of his hair. Slamming the door shut and shoving Will's body against it, he pushed his palm against Will's forehead, knocking it against the metal frame. Holding it there so Will would be unable to look away, the man said, "If you only hadn't gotten in my way. Actually," he said with a hideous laugh, "it wouldn't have mattered. Your fate would have been the same anyway."

Will, hoping to prolong his life, shot out a question. "What do you mean? Are you going to throw me to the ground and run me over with this car like you almost did last night?"

"I could. American brats deserve no better. But I plan on making you feel a little of the pain you and your country have given me."

With nothing to lose, Will asked, "How'd we bring you pain?"

The challenge made the man's face square into a grotesque smile. "So you want some answers, huh?" Pointing at the sliding right side of his face he continued, "You want to know how I got this?"

At that very moment, from the crunch of fallen tree vegetation came charging the muscular form of another man Will had asked answers of that day. Releasing his body into the air, Mr. Tenepior flew at the man like a battering ram. The man might have been able to miss the full blow if it hadn't been for the state of shock that overtook him.

With the slamming of his body, the man flew backwards. The force of the dive sent Tenepior rolling into a summersault over the man. Quickly each regained a fighting stance. The man had pulled up his knife from his side in the very same movement. With a swoop of his arm, he sent the blade slashing horizontally at Mr. Tenepior's chest.

Immediately shuffling to his left with a sidestep, Mr. Tenepior dodged the hacking blade. Using swift counter movements throwing his upper body to the left and right, he expertly made each thrust of the man's arm whiff through the air. Exploiting the man's momentum against him, Tenepior gripped both hands together and swung out at the same time. Like a homerun swing of a batter, his forearms exploded against the wrist holding the blade, leaving the arm with a pinpricking lifelessness. Thrusting out his foot, Tenepior's painful kick sunk into the man's gut. Instantaneously, he swung out with a left hook, catching the bent-over man on his deformed cheek, breaking through the skin and cracking his cheekbone. As the man fell backward, Mr. Tenepior did not relinquish his attack but charged toward him like a raging bull as the man struggled to stand.

Will watched in amazement as he slumped by the car, holding his wound. He had watched his share of shortstops make plays destined for highlight reels, but there was no comparison. This was pure athleticism and grace. He had never seen Mr. Tenepior move like that. In fact, he had never seen anyone move so expertly or forcibly.

All in one swift movement, Mr. Tenepior jabbed the man's throat with the back of his hand in a karate chopping motion and crosskicked the side of his right knee, buckling him backward to the ground with a cracking sound. Pouncing, he slammed his fist straight down into the center of the man's chest.

Barely being able to breathe, the man could only whimper. Tears streaming through his swollen eyes, his body went limp in unconsciousness. Rolling off him and shuffling toward Will, Mr. Tenepior snapped the tight bindings from Will's wrist with one quick easy tug. "Are you O.K.?"

"He cut me with his knife," Will coughed out, too surprised at the moment to really feel much of the pain. He managed to point to his side.

The whir of sirens could be heard coming toward them.

"Reinforcements. Help's coming." Mr. Tenepior nodded knowingly in the direction of the unnatural noise.

"How? How'd you?" Will stammered.

"I guess it's time I finally told you the truth," explained Mr. Tenepior.

Chapter 15

Pulling up behind them, two beige-colored unmarked cars skidded to a halt. Loose sand and tree needles swirled around the tires. Two men dressed in suit coats and wearing sunglasses stepped out of each vehicle. The man closest removed his pair of glasses and stepped forward. He wiped a bead of sweat from his forehead with a handkerchief. This movement looked so natural for the man that Will thought he must be used to being a second too late.

Peering up at the suited man, Mr. Tenepior spoke, "We need to take him back and have his side looked at. I'd guess he's going to need some stitches."

Reaching down with his arm, the man took Will's hand and hoisted him to his feet. Pulling Will to the rear door of the car with his left arm around his shoulders, he said, "You're a tough young man, Will. We'll get you back to normal in no time."

Reeling backward, Will couldn't figure out how in the world this man knew his name. As though he realized his mistake, the driver shot a glance at Mr. Tenepior.

Tenepior answered, "It's O.K." Redirecting his comments to Will, he continued, "Will, these men are big fans of yours." With that he opened the back door and slid in next to Will.

Reversing, the car soon found the highway. Two more cars followed, one being his teacher's silver Maxima. No one said anything for a long period of time as Will sat there looking sideways across the backseat with a hardened stare. Will saw for the first time a much greater depth to the man who was Mr. Tenepior. He had already felt firsthand his commanding presence and no-nonsense attitude, but he now witnessed a man no longer guarded by secrets.

Breaking the silence, Will blurted, "You're not just a teacher." He had meant it to be a question.

Looking up through the rearview mirror, the driver said, "The kid *is* good."

Nodding as if replying to both questions, Tenepior stared ahead. Turning his head toward Will, his mouth opened and then shut again as he lifted his shirt sleeve over his mouth to wipe his lips.

Sensing his trouble in answering, Will tried another question. "How'd you find me?" They drove for several miles as Will waited for a response.

"I got to thinking about what you said—about you seeing something at school," Mr. Tenepior finally stated. "I turned around and decided with everything going on, I'd better come back and check things out. As I pulled up in front of the building I saw some blood on the curb and you were nowhere around. There was only one car moving and it was racing along ahead. I sped around and chased after you to that spot in the trees."

Relieved, Will thought it was a good thing he had kept that maniac distracted. Sensing that Mr. Tenepior was speaking freely, Will pressed on. "Who are these guys?" nodding up toward the driver. "This isn't a police car we're riding in."

Through the rear-view mirror, Will saw the driver's eyes ask Mr. Tenepior the question, "How in the world are you going to explain this one?"

"In a second, you will find all your answers." This statement came with slowing of the vehicle. Will watched as Mr. Tenepior's Maxima pulled around and moved on past them. The car he was in cruised through a gate in a high voltage fence topped with razor wire and guarded by two armed soldiers. He could see a long brick building with similar nondescript vehicles parked alongside it.

Driving by what Will would have guessed was the main entrance, the driver pulled up to the far east wall of the building and through a set of warehouse doors as the second unmarked car pulled alongside. Without uttering another word, Mr. Tenepior got out of the car and came around to assist Will. Half carrying him through this open loading dock to a metal door, they stepped aside as other men came rushing out. Throwing open the door of the second car, two men roughly seized hold of the busted body of the unconscious man. Lugging the limp body by grabbing under his shoulders, they allowed his feet to drag across the cement and his head to hang loosely toward his chest. Looking at the beaten form, Will now knew why no students ever dared to cross his teacher.

Shuffling through the opening, Will was led past what looked like a jail cell before being helped into a large plain white-bricked room. Amidst a room lined with medical equipment, he sat down on the edge of a neatly fitted bed. Not quite understanding where he was, he watched as several people dressed like doctors strolled over to the bloody man's body. "Looks like he's suffered a crushed trachea and a possible collapsed lung," Will heard a white-coated man call out.

Also using his name, one doctor approached him, "Will, have a seat here while I examine the cut." Removing Will's shirt he said, "Yes, that's going to need some stitches." Peeking at a clipboard chart on which Will could see "Medical Records: Will Conlan," the doctor furiously scribbled notes. Will tried to take all of this in as he sat in confusion and looked back up at Mr. Tenepior.

"That man over there who cut you…" he paused, while Will took a long look at the man, "once led several successful attacks on our military troops in Iraq. He was one of the most wanted men in the world."

"What do you mean?"

"That man's name is Es Sayid. He is an Egyptian terrorist. We all thought he was dead. I thought he was dead. In fact, I'm the one who thought I had killed him."

Chapter 16

Fighting the doctor who was trying to make him lean over on his side, Will glanced up and struggled to listen hard to what Mr. Tenepior was now explaining. "He shot me once, in the back, of all places. Thought I had returned the favor. Presumed I had blown him to smithereens. I guess he somehow escaped the explosion. But by the look of his face, I definitely left a mark.

"And I guess that's why he didn't just run his truck into the stadium the other night and blow it up. I would say he had probably survived too much to be the suicide type."

Trying to sort through this segmented story, Will asked, "Who are you? What's all this?"

"A better question would be, how did I make it into your life?" Mr. Tenepior replied.

Will grimaced, not knowing if it was the needle or the question that stung more. Tenepior picked up a box off the floor and handed it to him. "Open it. The answers lie with what you're holding."

Feeling the tugs the doctor gave his stitches, Will tried to concentrate on the box by rolling it over in his hands. A small smile crept across Mr. Tenepior's face as he examined each of Will's movements. Will looked inside, around, and at the bottom of the box and then finally looked up. Giving Mr. Tenepior back his own reflected grin, he ran his hands around the outer edges of the box and said, "Our best thinking happens out here." Knowing the school lesson well, Will said, "O.K. So that's your teaching philosophy. What's that got to do with everything else?"

Getting the nod from the doctor, Mr. Tenepior said, "Follow me. I have something to show you." Will reached for his shirt, but was handed a brand new t-shirt by a man who had just entered the room. Realizing that his old shirt had been ruined by his his gashing wound and blood stain, he painfully pulled the new one over his head and slid off the table. Shocked to find the new shirt identical in size, brand, and design to his old one, Will enclosed his hands around a cardboard tag at the neck line. He tugged at the plastic fastener and yanked the price tag apart as he wondered if it had just been purchased.

Following Tenepior down a long hallway and through a set of iron-reinforced doors, Will spotted a wide network of computer terminals and screens that lined each wall and displayed surveillance footage of people, events, and even the weather. Above all these, hanging from a set of wires, was a banner that read in huge italicized bold letters, *"We paint a picture where there are no dots to connect."*

Following Mr. Tenepior into a large office, Will was suddenly struck with amazement stronger than any blow he had received that day. Inside the room pinned to bulletin boards were classroom photos, newspaper clippings, and notes all detailing the life of Will Conlan. On a corner of the desk, papers written in his own handwriting were organized neatly with sticky notes plastered at odd angles. Three separate monitors showed angles of his own home and computer screen in his very bedroom.

Walking over to the center of the display, Will noticed the sports page clipping of his rosin bag throw. That's when Mr. Tenepior chose to fill in the gaps. "That's what started it all." He paused with a far-off gaze as if reliving some fond memory.

Not feeling like his questions were being answered quickly enough, Will cut in. "I know you're not some sort of sports' agent."

Raising one eyebrow, Mr. Tenepior flatly continued, "Will, I work for the CIA." He once again paused as if he wanted his point to sink in. "After being injured in the line of duty, I was transferred to the Homeland Security division of the Central Intelligence Agency. By special appointment, the director placed me at a desk here in the Homeland Security's Analytic Red Cell and gave me the duty of compiling data on terrorists and their movements across the nation, as well as the special task of deciphering their forms of communication.

"I played a large role in getting the *NewsFocus Tonight* special on the air." Adding a little disgruntled hint, he continued, "The news program that *you* were supposed to watch." Will's gaze shifted to the floor. "As that program discussed, we employed all strategies and technologies at our disposal, but we were still falling short. Every idea our Red Teamers came up with ran into complications. The terrorists were always two steps ahead. They were original thinkers."

He paused as if he were reliving each separate moment. Showing a sign of grief and frustration, he walked over to his desk, leaned hard on his whitened knuckles, and continued, "We had been struggling for months trying to solve all sorts of problems dealing with terrorism in America. Take 9/11 for instance. The Red Cell had contingency plans to counteract their bomb making schemes. We had collected information on attacking targets such as the Pentagon or even the World Trade Center. We even had plans for their hijacking planes. But we lacked the original thinking to stop them from using a plane *as* a bomb to attack these places. We needed to think like them. Our ideas were too conventional. They were all based on probabilities. We were like an elephant—we had four knees, but we couldn't jump."

Pulling himself upright and walking to the corner near a whitewashed marker board, he continued, "We went as far as asking for some creative problem solving from philosophers, futurists, and even big Hollywood movie writers when we realized that their movies were a better representation of actual terrorist plots. With the surge of recent attacks on our soil, we had to act quickly or become overrun."

Mr. Tenepior gestured toward the banner in the main operations hall. "I truly believe in what Jon Nowick, the director of the Analytic Red Cell program, said about painting pictures where there are no dots, but we were in desperate need of more pictures painted."

Raising his arm and pointing to the wall with the bulletin board Will was still staring at, he said, "Seeing that very article about your baseball play gave me an idea. You did something in baseball that had never been done before. Your inventiveness as a playmaker was a very 'outside the box' idea. It was just the type of thinking we were so in need of.

"Pursuing our idea, we quickly found that our assertions were very much true. Kids have very active imaginations. They are not clouded by the premise of 'it can't be done.' They don't have a full grasp of the complications of life or exactly how it works, so their thinking does not get bogged down with these hindrances."

Mr. Tenepior pulled the lanyard still holding his teacher ID over his head and wrapped it around a map hook atop the whiteboard. "That's when I became your new English teacher. Yes, I came to your school specifically to exploit your way of thinking. Utilizing a highly trained staff in this very room, we created a whole series of lesson plans directed at searching out original 'out of the box' thinking from students. Incorporating grade-appropriate literature and writing lessons, we keyed on connecting our problems with the conflicts found in young adult literature."

"So that's why you have us watch the news so much and read stories where old women light fire to themselves," Will broke in as if completing a puzzle.

"Yes. It's been time consuming, but, after today, I think totally worth all the trouble."

Trouble. Had Tenepior meant him and today or all the teaching? Will, finally grasping the truth of what he was hearing, said, "That's why I saw you running out of school last Monday."

"I was obviously needed elsewhere when the terrorists attacked."

Feeling oddly like a celebrity with so much attention focused on him, Will asked, "What am I going to tell my parents?"

"It's already been taken care of. They think you are with me working after hours on a school project."

"You guys think of everything," Will retorted.

"That's our job, but obviously we need some help at times." Mr. Tenepior allowed himself a little chuckle.

Will, pushing forward, asked, "So I take it we got him and life can go back to normal?"

"Actually he's only one of many. There's a long road in front of us. The Red Cell still needs your help. I promise no more knives. Are you with us?" Mr. Tenepior asked.

Taking a moment to consider all that he had already done and what he could be missing with a life like this, he replied, "Us? I'm still not totally sure who you really are."

"That was the one thing that has been real all along. My name's actually Mark Tenepior. Will, let me put it to you this way. We had great success today. We think you solved a major piece of the puzzle. But we still have a long way to go. We need your help to stop them while we have the upper hand."

Feeling like the upper hand at this moment might be his, Will was bold enough to say, "There are some questions I'd like to have answered."

"O.K., shoot away."

"Can I go back to school?"

"Of course. Life will be just like normal, except for any time you spend here."

"Is this kept secret or can I tell people?"

"No one can know. You will not be able to tell anyone. Not your parents, certainly not Ryan, and definitely not your girlfriend."

Stacey! Will's mind reeled. It was the first time all evening he had thought about her. He was astonished that his mind had managed to block her out for so long; it had to have been a record for him. Not understanding how Mr. Tenepior knew about their relationship, he suddenly blushed for a second.

"We have been watching you very closely," he said, apparently noticing Will's reaction. "But if you agree to help us, we will agree to remove any surveillance of your home so you can feel normal."

Not even considering those options yet, Will plugged, "Stacey doesn't want anything to do with me after you made me out to be crazy in class today. You have to ease up on me from now on and say something to correct what you said in front of everyone."

"Will, I don't think that would be wise. I feel pretty confident that I was able to make them believe that none of it could be true. We already talked about what would happen if your classmates thought it all possible."

Not budging, Will crossed his arms and sat still. Finally, Tenepior broke and said, "I'll do whatever I can."

Will, having heard that line from him before and knowing it to be true, asked, "For how long?"

"We really need you for one last mission. We have to figure out a way to stop the very people who are planning these attacks."

Chapter 17

Bursting with enthusiasm and energy from the newly found knowledge he carried, Will walked through the hallways of school as if he had been resurrected. Though he could tell no one of his new secret status, he felt an importance for why he was there. Now realizing the value of the thinking skills he was developing, he understood a connectedness between what he was learning and the greater life beyond those school walls.

Once again looking from face to face of his fellow students, Will saw the same look of uncertainty dulled by a day's repetition. He wanted to scream out, to stand up and yell, "Look at me. I've done something extraordinary." He didn't feel like any of the zoned-out zombies shuffling from classroom to classroom. He had done something important. Something no one would know about—a secret. A secret that lives depended on. It was a far cry from the rejection he had felt from his classmates the day before.

Knowing that Mr. Tenepior had given his word to heal those scars left behind from yesterday's mocking, his hand went under his shirt to his side and gingerly retraced the jagged stitches, his secret clue to a new life's role. A sharp stab of pain as he took his seat for English class was a reminder of how far he had come and the direction in which he was headed.

Mr. Tenepior calmed things down with his booming voice, "Today your assignment was to finish reading the story *Holes* by Louis Sachar. Part III of this particular story is entitled 'Filling in the Holes.' In relation to the story, I want you to consider what additional meaning this section heading holds. What further understanding can we gain from this message?"

Looking around the room, Will saw that each student was busy treating this class period like any other day. Taking out notepaper and busily jotting down ideas, the students responded with a flurry of thoughts. He hadn't really expected Mr. Tenepior to come out directly with an apology. He knew this man would not be able to choke such words out of his mouth, but the discussion seemed to be taking much more time than he had hoped. He wanted some acknowledgement for doing something good. He felt like he deserved it. He wanted to see the looks on their faces, changed looks from the giggling grins surrounding him yesterday. He wanted Stacey's approval. He waited for a change in the discussion's direction where a promise would be fulfilled.

After hearing all of the connections made from the story, Mr. Tenepior stated, "One hole that still needs to be filled in is deciding what we can learn from the *mistaken* ideas that came out in yesterday's discussion. Although we examined how all of that could not be true," Mr. Tenepior paused and cleared out his throat as Will shot him an angry glance. Mr. Tenepior continued, "I thought it might be worthwhile to examine the possibilities such a theory about commercials might carry. I want you all today to consider the effects of advertising on the shaping of our beliefs."

Will buried his head in his hands. This was not quite what he had wanted Tenepior to say. He had been hoping that Mr. Tenepior would credit him for his thinking to help ease the embarrassment he had already suffered. Frustrated, he pondered the possibility of giving Tenepior an earful later that night at headquarters.

Pressing the power button to the LCD projector, Mr. Tenepior played a recorded series of commercials. Flashing images splattered the vinyl screen. "Pay special attention to the devices these advertisers use to make their viewers feel they want such a product. What's their message and how do they get it across? Who is their targeted audience and how do you know? What gimmicks are they using? How do they play on your emotions?"

Mr. Tenepior continued his instruction, asking his students to interpret the messages being sent to them through coordinated audio and visual means. Finishing with an outdated C2 commercial flooded with dancing office workers and the high-spirited frolics of teenagers, the students easily connected its purpose to the accompanying song blaring the lyrics, "I want to break free."

Will listened as his classmates interpreted meaning from what they saw and heard. He appreciated how his teacher had deftly managed to empower each student to explore his own thinking while occasionally planting an idea or two of his own into the conversation. Slowly, as the discussion progressed, Mr. Tenepior showed how susceptible people are to slogans that continually pound their message into the minds of their watchers. Will watched as Mr. Tenepior skillfully wound his way as though directing traffic, diverting this discussion back to brainstorming about using the media to counteract terrorist possibilities. For the first time, Will noted how cleverly the lesson plans were contrived not only to teach a concept, but also to explore the ideas his agency was after.

"Now, if such media were able even to make a believer out of our Will," Tenepior paused as Will cringed, knowing his classmates were remembering his supposed bungle, "how could we use that against them?"

A prolonged silence fogged across the classroom. Mr. Tenepior rephrased his question. "O.K., let's suppose for one second that Will had been correct. How could we use the knowledge of how they communicate against the ones making the plans?"

Alan, sitting in his usual rear corner seat, raised his hand with a snicker. Will figured this humor must have lingered from yesterday's verbal lashing. "Presuming Will had been right…correct?" Alan paused, looking around the classroom for the backup of agreeing chuckles, then blurted out the obvious, "We wait for the next commercial and catch them in the act."

"Thank you for such insightful thinking, Alan," Mr. Tenepior said, regaining his usual sarcastic tone. Pulling an empty desk around and seating himself on top of it to face his class, he said, "Let's try to think of strategies that our government wouldn't have already employed."

Kyle raised his hand. "Nobody knows who's doing this, right?" Waiting to get nods from people, he continued, "Somebody's probably dying to get credit for the attacks." Will sharply looked up, sensing that Kyle had somehow read his mind and tapped into his longing for some credit. "I mean, why couldn't the government just get a bunch of terrorist-looking guys on TV and have them lie about setting up the attacks, saying they were the ones who did it? The real planners would get in a hissy fit and start announcing who they really are so they can have credit for the bombing. After that our government could pounce on them."

Getting all over Kyle's idea, Brenda remarked, "Terrorist-looking guys?" giving a different type of pouncing than what Kyle had probably meant.

Ignoring Brenda's comment, and following up on Kyle's proposal, Steven put in his two cents worth. "Or we could have them filmed giving up. If their fellow attackers are giving up left and right, it'll take the heart out of them."

While taking a few notes of his own, Mr. Tenepior said, "These are all good ideas. There are some flaws with those thoughts, though. One, our government couldn't just film anyone. These people probably know or have worked with each other, so just showing some generic person wouldn't mean much."

Cutting Mr. Tenepior off, Ryan threw in an idea of his own. "Why couldn't we wait for the next commercial, stop the attackers, and fake the attack like it really happened? Our government could use special effects with computer graphics to make it look like a bomb blew something up. The news people like my mom could show the fake footage on TV. While the planners of the attack are distracted with success, we could trace the original Treks tape sent to the TV studios back through internet channels and get them."

The second Ryan had mentioned seeing the next commercial, Will realized everyone in this class might still find out his theory was true. He hadn't thought of that. By the look in his eyes, Mr. Tenepior had just realized the same thing. "Sounds like a very complicated plan. I'm not sure our government would be able to carry it out so quickly, let alone receive such cooperation with the press. That is, though, more along the lines of the type of thinking I like."

With that statement, Stacey, shot a possibility of her own. "Why couldn't our government make a Treks commercial of its own to show during the next Cubs' game? It could give whatever clues they want, maybe showing that the terrorists all need to have a big meeting somewhere. When they all show up, it would give the police a chance to get them."

A silence spread across the room as everyone considered Stacey's impressive plan. Will stared at Stacey as though she were the most perfect female in existence. He had actually already decided that, but this just confirmed it for him.

Glancing back, her eyes rested on his. With that flash of her eyes, Will realized how hard she had been pondering all that had happened between the two of them, what he had done, and whether or not she was going to forgive him. With a yearning heart he wanted to race over and tell her everything—to show her how he had not made a fool out of himself. He wanted her to be proud of his doing something wonderful.

He could even strip off his shirt and show her the proof. But Tenepior would never allow it. He would not be able to say anything.

Will, getting frustrated because Tenepior had skirted his apology by masking it too subtly, shouted out, "I heard the CIA apprehended a terrorist last night."

A fierce burning anger flashed across Mr. Tenepior's face. "No, I hadn't heard that, Will." His name was spat out as if it were a warning.

Not really wanting to give any vital information away, Will stated his proposal, "Why couldn't the CIA force this suspect into recording a message saying he had been captured and was going to plea bargain his way down by naming names of his fellow terrorists. Like the world's greatest fake-out, they could show that on the news and all connected terrorists would probably go running. The CIA could then catch them trying to leave the country."

Nodding his head vigorously as he tilted his chin to look back at Will, Kyle slapped his hand down on his desk and immediately burst out with his well-known version of Tenepior's favorite saying, "Yah, we'll blow smoke up their…"

Quickly cutting him off before Kyle could say something that would get him in trouble, Will completed the thought for him, "Just like you taught us. Show smoke, let the reader infer fire."

Chapter 18

As class was dismissed, Will stepped around desks in an effort to catch Stacey. He met her head-on as she had lingered in the hall.

"I didn't mean to spoil the other night," he apologetically offered.

A faint crease of her dimple showed signs of a smile, but before she could reply, Mr. Tenepior's voice rose to cut in. "Mr. Conlan, I need to see you for a second ASAP."

Turning to look from one to the other, Will allowed disappointment to cloud his expression. Grabbing his hand, Stacey pushed a square folded piece of paper into his palm. Clasping the note, he turned toward Tenepior as she sauntered away. He had really wanted to speak to Stacey, but before he had a chance, Tenepior placed his hand behind his shoulder and ushered him to follow out the back door.

"Your outburst in class wasn't very smart, Will, but once again your idea may just be the angle we have been searching for. We've got to get to headquarters and start working on Es Sayid."

As he opened the passenger side door, Will interjected, "How come it seems like I keep holding up my end of the deal, but you didn't say one thing in class today like you promised you were going to."

"If you want me to come out and explain what really happened and make you some sort of hero in front of your friends, then you can forget it," replied Tenepior as he slammed the door shut.

"You said…"

"I said that I'd do my best. Did I not treat your ideas with the utmost respect today? Did I not come back to your theory as if it sounded reasonable to me?"

"Forget it," said Will sullenly. He knew that Tenepior would not jeopardize this investigation in any way. Remaining silent the rest of the way, Will tried to consider just how he was going to make it up to both Ryan and Stacey.

As they rounded the corner heading down the street leading to the substation, Will noticed a whole curbside of news reporters crowded outside screaming questions at a suited man who was trying to retain some order. Tenepior's hand shot out and slammed Will's head downward. "Get down!"

Will's eyes still had managed to catch eight or nine news vehicles parked inside the gates. One van even had a camera elevated from its roof filming an aerial shot of the building and crowd. He wondered if Ryan's mom was in the crowd of reporters. Clearly upset, Mr. Tenepior blamed, "Did you know about this?"

"No," Will shot back defensively.

"You didn't say anything to Ryan, did you?" he questioned accusingly.

"Nothing."

Without looking back at the scene, Tenepior accelerated forward. "Can't allow anyone to see either of us. Now we'll have to use the other entrance. No one's to know we have anything to do with this place. Do I make myself clear?" he ordered as if he didn't really believe Will after his bringing up the arrested terrorist in class.

"What other entrance?" asked Will.

"Well, I suppose if you are going to be working with us, there are a few things you should know." As he said this, he sped past the shouting bunch around the compound to a small scattering of quaint houses rounding out a residential area. Opening up the door to a mailbox tamped into the ground next to the roadside curb, Tenepior typed in a series of numbers on a keypad welded to the opened hatch. Secretly Will watched his fingers type 5663. At that very instant, the garage door facing the driveway in front of them rolled upward, folding its sectionals toward the garage's ceiling. Leaving his driver's side window down and pulling the Maxima to a halt under a single light bulb, Mr. Tenepior stretched through his open window and once again typed the combination into a different keypad affixed to the center of the wall some four feet from the ground. Retracting backwards, the rotating panels unfolded downwards, shutting out the afternoon's light. Humming a vibrating pulse, the car lurched and Will reached for the safety handles above the car's door. He felt himself falling. Peering through the windshield, Will watched the walls disappear to reveal steel shafts pulling them into some secret underground facility.

Seeing Will's astonishment, Mr. Tenepior said with a slight grin "Well, we are in the business of secrets."

After they came to a stop, Tenepior opened his door and said, "Follow me."

Will could see another vehicle parked behind a steel girder far down the basement garage. Solid cement sectionals divided the opposite wall. Here and there a storage box occupied a corner. The whole room was so plain that it resembled some elaborate janitor's closet minus the brooms and mops.

Throwing his thumb over his shoulder, Mr. Tenepior remarked, "You like my parking spot, huh? It's technically been mine for the using since I had to go undercover as your teacher. Wasn't worth the risk of anyone connecting my vehicle to both places."

Stepping below a line of fluorescent lights, they made their way back to the substation. Peering down to the far southern end of the basement, Will asked, "What's with all the equipment?"

Pointing to the row of power generators against one wall for clarification, he replied, "That's what powers the whole facility. They're kept here so no outside person can tamper with them."

Taking note of every fascinating step he took, Will memorized their route, realizing that this was much more than some school tour could provide. Walking to a perfectly curved dead end and stopping, Mr. Tenepior said, "Squeeze toward me."

Although he felt a little queasy standing that close to his teacher, Will knew Tenepior wasn't going to wait around for his direction to be followed. Tenepior grabbed a small notch in the sidewall and pulled sideways with his arm. The whole wall rotated 180 degrees around like a darkroom door to reveal a staircase before them. Mr. Tenepior pointed upwards as a square slot in the ceiling above them slid backward, exposing a lighted room above. Unable to close his gaping mouth, Will sprinted up the steps and found himself standing squarely adjacent to the solid oak desk in Tenepior's office. With a faint smile tracing his lips, Tenepior leaned over and whispered, "Rarely do you want to leave yourself without options."

Looking around, Will's eyes immediately fell on the glass shelving on the other side of the desk. Because of his state of shock the day before, he hadn't noticed the display cabinet. Resembling a high school's trophy case, the four shelves held a well-organized collection of James Bond-looking paraphernalia. There appeared to be an arsenal of devices from night vision goggles and camera equipment to a smoke grenade and different types of uniforms. He even suspected there might be a cigarette gun in there somewhere.

Obviously pleased with Will's fascination in his personal collection, Mr. Tenepior stated, "Those are all sorts of spy relics. You'll find Seismic Intruder Detection Devices that look like stones, samples of microscopic film, and a 'Belly Buster' hand drill. That's the *real* James Bond equipment."

Mr. Tenepior cut the conversation short. The office door opened as several men, seemingly not at all astonished to see them standing there, walked into the room and sat down. Ready to quickly discuss the new contingency plan devised during class, one man began rewinding a digital image flashing across one of the screens lining the wall and pressed play. Will stared in disbelief as the SMART Board projected his entire class arguing about how they would use commercials. Rehearing all that was said by each of his fellow classmates, a few of the agents in the room mumbled to one another. Several eyes were on him. Will got the feeling that they had already seen this footage. Pausing the recording after Will's statement about capturing the terrorist, Tenepior refocused his eyes on Will and said, "What's with all the camera crews out front?" as if still implying that he thought Will had something to do with it.

A tall and rather burly man spoke, "We had to announce the capture. National Security Team was anxious to show the public that we are making some progress in our fight for their safety. They want the people to know the success this administration is having in our combat against terror."

Will tried his best to flash the same stern, squinting look back at Mr. Tenepior in self-satisfaction of the explanation.

"All is well. It may have given us the chance to employ Will's new strategy." Tenepior hit the resume button from his own handheld PC. The interactive whiteboard flickered Will's image raising his hand and stating his plan to the class. Working quickly, each agent started discussing this proposal of creating the news brief involving their new captive giving up the names of all his helpers.

While they furiously jotted down ideas and traded their technical expertise, one man with snow-white hair hobbled over on unsteady legs and handed an envelope to Will. He whispered, "In all the years we served in the Special Forces together, Mark never asked me for a favor quite like this. He wanted you to have these. It took some arm-twisting to get them."

Grabbing the envelope and quickly opening it, Will found four tickets to Sunday's Cubs' playoff game against the Atlanta Braves. With all that he had been through since Wednesday, Will had nearly forgotten that the win he had missed had clinched a playoff berth for the Cubs. Looking up at Mr. Tenepior with an overjoyed expression, he couldn't help but be filled with excitement. Secretly Will knew that Mark Tenepior was a man of his word and had tried his best to make it all up to him. Bending toward the man, Will asked, "Is there somewhere private I could use a phone?" The man nodded, pointing down the hall.

Slipping out the door, Will passed two large rooms containing high-tech digital graphing equipment. Some displayed maps with sketched in routes and targets. He shook his head knowing that the surveillance equipment at home and in his classroom was a far cry from all these people really could do. Finding a vacant office room, Will lifted a phone to give his dad a call. Mr. Tenepior had already told his father that he would have him back home before dinner, but Will had to ask his father if he would like to go to Sunday afternoon's game. Suddenly considering all four tickets, Will knew Tenepior had thought of his friends. Reaching into his pocket, he pulled out Stacey's note for the first time. Unfolding it, he saw just a few words sketched in her curvy handwriting. It said, "Call me."

It couldn't have been more ideal. Not only did she want to talk to him, but he had a great way to make it all up to her. Perfect date attempt number two. After speaking to his father, who quickly agreed to going, he dialed Stacey's number.

After listening to Will's awkward apology, Stacey was hesitant to say yes. "I don't know if I'm ready for that again, Will."

"Please let me make it up to you. There's no one I'd rather watch that game with." There was a long silence on the line. He begged with a pleading "Please."

"Tell me that you'll promise that you won't do anything crazy this time."

Slowly letting the ashamed words fall from his lips, he replied, "I promise I won't do anything crazy this time."

"Promise?"

"Yes, I promise."

"Then say it again."

"I promise I won't do anything crazy this time."

"In that case, I'd love to go," she said.

Next, he had to give Ryan a call. He knew that Ryan was still mad at him for missing the end of the game a couple of nights before. Maybe this invitation would turn him around. Will couldn't imagine Ryan passing up a ticket to a playoff game no matter how mad he was.

After hanging up the phone, Will was once again filled with excitement. He was ready to help Tenepior in any way he could. Walking back into the room, he noticed no one was talking. Many were holding their hands to their heads. One man was walking small circles quietly talking to himself. Seeing Will walk in, Mr. Tenepior said, "Es Sayid won't talk. They tried all day to get any information out of him and he wouldn't say a word about any of it."

Unable to let the thought pass, Will chortled, "Maybe you hit him too hard?" That raised the heads of most of the operatives in the office. Will knew of only one who had served in combat with Tenepior, but the rest had recently seen the damage he could cause.

Ignoring the comment, Tenepior replied, "Your plan won't work. We had to go back to the drawing board."

Still riding the emotional high of the tickets, Will pointed his finger to lightheartedly poke fun at all the scratched-out scribbles marking the SMART Board screen. "I thought you believed in *painting* pictures." He watched as the eyes of most of the operatives flicked back and forth between him and Tenepior.

It was apparent to Will that Mr. Tenepior had dealt with his fair share of teenagers as he stood unfazed by his sarcasm. Deciding from the gloomy silence of the room that he must have been the only one lucky enough to have been given tickets, he continued, "O.K. Here's an idea. I saw all that computer and camera equipment next to the main operations area. Why couldn't we do what Ryan suggested today in class?"

Flipping through his yellow pad, Mr. Tenepior shook his head no. "That plan had way too many flaws in it."

"No. That's not what I meant. We could use that equipment to make a virtual Es Sayid. We could program him to say whatever we want."

The white haired man was first to respond. "That might actually work. We already spent the day filming Es Sayid. We can easily digitize his face by transferring the images over to the digital graphing equipment."

Another agent pointed out, "All we would need is to get him to say something to get a sample of his speech patterns."

Always business-like, Tenepior cut in, "Can we have this developed in time to show during tomorrow night's opening playoff game?"

While diligently gnawing on the shaft of his pencil, an agent who had noticeably been mulling all this over stated, "If you can get him to talk, it won't be a problem."

Open-mouthed, the rest of the team started hurriedly moving. Picking up papers and darting out the door, they seemed convinced the plan would work and wanted to get started.

Will overheard one man who was exiting say, "Man, that kid can think like a terrorist." Puzzling over whether or not that had actually been a compliment, Will raised his eyebrows.

The man who had brought him the tickets leaned over and slapped his back. "I'm glad you're on our side, Will." Smiling, he grabbed the cane hooked to the back of his chair and departed the room leaving only Mr. Tenepior and Will alone.

Tenepior spoke first, "Sounds like your work here is done for today. We better get you home before your parents begin to wonder what's happened to you."

"I already called them. Had to ask Dad if he could take us to the game Sunday. Thanks for the tickets."

"You just go and enjoy the game. You deserve it."

"So do you think we'll get them?" asked Will.

Tenepior replied, "We'll just have to see what type of video we can make by tomorrow night's game."

Chapter 19

Forty-five minutes later, Will's father met him at the door of his home. Excitedly, he asked to see the tickets for himself and ushered Will to the kitchen where supper was waiting. With one raised eyebrow, he shot a questioning glace toward Will, "Don't suppose this game will be nearly as exciting as the last one you went to." It was a statement, not a question.

Will wasn't sure what his father meant by that. Had Mr. Moritz told him the full story? Would his father object to his going to this game? Trying to show that he could definitely be trusted to behave at the game, Will said, "Can't wait to watch every second of it!"

Will noticed that his parents had anxiously been waiting for him; they had already set out the entire meal on the table. Lifting the tinfoil off a corner of his plate, he noticed that it was already a little cold.

"Sorry you had to wait for me. This school work's taking a lot of time to complete."

"Mr. Tenepior seems to assign an awful lot of lengthy projects," his father stated.

"Yeah, but he did give me the tickets for working so hard on it lately," Will replied, hoping his father wouldn't decide that it was time for him to readjust his priorities.

"That was very nice of him," said his mother. "I wonder how a man on his salary can get tickets like that?"

Splashed with an instant cold sweat, Will busied his fork separating the peas from the potatoes, hoping he wouldn't be forced to come up with some explanation. Cutting in, his father suggested, "I'm guessing there's much more to this Mr. Tenepior than one would think."

Choking on the mouthful of food he had stuffed in his mouth, Will reached for his glass of orange juice. His father picked his plate up to reheat his dinner in the microwave oven. As if he had made up his mind, he muttered, "Well I'm sure it'll be worth it in the long run."

His father didn't know the half of it.

"Oh, it definitely will be. I promise."

This was bound to be a memorable weekend. Not only were the Cubs in the playoffs, but a plan he thought of would be aired on TV sometime during Saturday night's opening playoff game against the Braves. The entire Red Cell had anticipated that this would be the perfect time to show the video recording. Surely the terrorists would be watching the very broadcast they had been using. When they were caught, he would be a national hero.

This thought continued to delight his dreams. Wonderful nightlong stories involving his heroic efforts to stop terrorism filled his deep sleep. Parades lined the streets as crowds cheered wildly. He was invited to throw out the first pitch at the World Series. The ballplayers carried him around the stadium on their shoulders. Stacey publicly swore her love and dedication for him. All these sweet dreams contributed to the best sleep he had experienced in several weeks.

His excitement continued throughout Saturday. That evening, waiting for the game to begin, Will's legs shook the couch with his nervous bouncing. Tonight the meal was served on TV trays. Positioned around the entire living room, his family was ready to cheer on their team. With a call from the kitchen, his mother signaled, "Come fix your plates." Getting up to follow his dad to the kitchen, he could barely stand all the night's excitement. Choosing to heat his sandwich, he placed it in the microwave oven. Just as the timer ended with a ding, the TV cut out abruptly and switched over to a news brief.

"This just in. Breaking news about the recent terrorist attacks in Chicago. Continuing coverage of the game will follow this announcement," sounded the refined voice of the lead anchor. Hustling over to peek around the corner of the room, both Will and his dad gazed at the TV. Will smiled slyly, knowing all too well what the breaking news would be about. "Yesterday we broke the story that Es Sayid, a terrorist suspected to be directly involved in the attack on the Sears Tower, had been apprehended and was being questioned by the CIA. Apparently those interrogations were successful. The video that follows comes directly from the Homeland Security post here in Chicago."

Moving over to the couch for a better view, Will and his dad excitedly sat to listen to the brief. On the screen came the scarred face of a man whose fire-filled eyes burned into the camera. The man cleared his throat to speak. Through the harsh tone Will all too clearly recognized, Es Sayid fiercely called out, spitting a spray of saliva with his chant, "I am Es Sayid. I am being held prisoner for terroristic attacks on the city of Chicago."

The breathy scratchiness of the voice sounded just like the real Es Sayid. In fact, Will wasn't sure that this wasn't actually him. The computer-generated graphics captured every single crispy burnt fold of his face and mimicked his grim hatred-filled scowl perfectly. If he hadn't known the plan, Will would have been completely fooled about the actual identity of the image now staring out of the screen directly at him. Knowing he had been thoroughly questioned by Tenepior on their way home about Es Sayid's rantings when Will had been kidnapped, he couldn't wait to hear what they had programmed this computer representation of the man to say.

Adding confirmation of his identity, the voice said, "I was captured while carrying out our last mission just days ago—a great plan of revenge for your country's actions. You Americans have no idea what your own self-righteous country has done to my people. I bare the scars of such atrocities!

"We seek to inflict equal brutality on the ones who did the same to us. No longer can the United States impose its will as it pleases. We shall set the human race free of your control—your corruption—and the world will see us as heroes. It is time everyone knows exactly who we are and the rest of the world can thank us."

Once again the screen cut out to an astonished gaping mouth of the news reporter who had obviously not been allowed the time to see the recording previously. Will felt much the same way as he slapped his thigh with utter glee, unable to hold back the excited smile that spread across his face. His pulse thumped like a drum roll. Thoroughly impressed with the whole production, he considered how ingenious it was to cover Es Sayid naming terrorists under the guise of wanting to publicize his cause. And the message was ambiguous enough to allow the CIA to make it seem authentic. It couldn't have been more perfect.

Continuing to talk, the anchor reiterated that Es Sayid, an Egyptian terrorist presumed to be connected to the bombing of the Sears Tower, had been apprehended. "In a stunning video, we have just heard the first testimony as to the motive of these terrorists. We are told further reports detailing the specific individuals behind the attacks and their motives are to follow in the next few days as the CIA investigates the validity of his comments. Data is being compiled about the men Es Sayid has named to the authorities and will be posted to websites in hopes that anyone with information on the listed suspects may immediately contact the CIA.

"We now have Dr. Thomas Holmes, a professor of criminal justice at the University of Illinois joining us. Dr. Holmes, as an expert on terrorism, what are your initial thoughts on Es Sayid's comments?"

"One has to guess that once captured," began the professor, "Es Sayid saw divulging this information as his only hope of continuing his cause. It is not surprising for a terrorist cell to seek media avenues to publicize their objectives or grievances. His motives may include embarrassing the government or just media attention in the hopes others will join the fight. As long as he is spreading fear, he is accomplishing his goal."

"Professor, do you think Es Sayid could be hurting his own cause? Wouldn't you agree that learning these identities gives the American people more optimism than fear?"

"You have to realize that there's great fear created by his *confirming* there are others just like him living in our neighborhoods ready to do us harm."

"But shouldn't Es Sayid be concerned that surely our authorities will do everything in their power to search, find, and detain each one of his fellow terrorists?"

"Not if you're Es Sayid! This man has successfully avoided capture for years. In fact, our government had him listed as deceased. I'm sure he is confident in their elusiveness. Though, in my opinion, overly confident now that he's been captured."

Speaking above the professor's voice, Will's dad shot him a knowing glance. "See, Son. That's why you can't let your imagination get the better of you. That terrorist is in custody. They've probably had him for days."

Will's mother spoke up, "What's all this about?"

"Oh, nothing. It's just something that Robert Moritz and I were discussing tonight on the phone about the ball game Will went to," Will's dad said, masking the complete truth. Will knew his dad did not want to frighten his mother with a complete account of that night's events, but was letting his son know that he was fully aware of the stunt Will had pulled.

Will could have cared less at this very moment. It had all been worth it. Those terrorists would have to run now. If they were caught and nobody else got hurt, then he could easily handle a hundred nights of embarrassment and ridicule. Looking over at his father he replied, "I'm just glad he's caught." Wanting to show his father that he could still be trusted to behave, he added, "Should make it easier to concentrate on tomorrow's game."

After the news flash that took up nearly a half-hour's time, the game resumed. For the first time in his life, Will felt like he might almost want to watch the news even more than he wanted to see the game. But that thought quickly diminished as the fast-moving game had already entered the top of the fourth inning.

As with most typical Cubs' games, the team hadn't yet managed to knock in any runners to home. They were down by three runs to Atlanta. As he watched the screen, his mind swirled excitedly with the thoughts of the television video of Es Sayid. It was scary to think about just how quickly everything had happened. It was also somewhat unnerving to consider that tomorrow he would be back in the same place where only a few days before he had almost been killed.

Suddenly feeling thirsty, he leapt from the couch and went to the kitchen for a drink. After closing the refrigerator door, he heard the unmistakable voice that had haunted his thoughts. "*Treks!*" With a swift alertness, he swiveled, craning his neck to see the TV.

On the screen flashed a view of the Navy Pier. It showed a pickpocket stealing a woman's purse, jumping the guardrail of the walkway, and landing on a motorboat where he sped away through the water. Glancing up at the disturbance, a bystander who was receiving his change back from a cotton candy stand dropped they money to the ground and raced to the rescue. In a sprint, the man leapt up to the first seat on the giant spinning Ferris wheel in the middle of the pier and jumped from carriage to carriage, gaining momentum with each leap. With one last burst as his body reached the pinnacle of the sphere, he vaulted from the highest seat. Landing with a crash on the wooden deck, he stood on top of the thief. Zooming in, the camera focused on a brand new Treks sneaker pinning the villain's head to the boat's floorboards. While flashing a thumbs-up sign, a voice responded, "*Treks!* What trek will they lead you on? Coming soon to a store near you."

Will couldn't believe what he had just witnessed. Were the terrorists planning another attack? How could they after seeing the news brief? Trying to inhale breaths slowly to calm down, Will realized that the commercial would have been sent to the TV station way before any terrorists could have seen the news flash. But how in the world could they be planning another attack now? Hadn't they noticed Es Sayid was missing? Overexcited all day, his jittery feelings turned to nervousness as he quickly mowed down the corners of his fingernails. Maybe the terrorists hadn't even seen the news flash. And with a second thought, he considered that possibly Tenepior hadn't seen this commercial either.

Excusing himself from the game to the dismayed looks on his parents' faces, Will ran up the stairs to call the phone number Mr. Tenepior had given him. When Tenepior finally picked up his office phone, Will blurted out, "Did you see the commercial?"

Cutting in, Mr. Tenepior replied, "Yes, Will, we all were watching. Lately it seems as if everyone in the whole agency has become Cubs' fans."

"What do you think they'll do?"

"Too soon to tell, but every available agent will be undercover at the pier. We'll be on the lookout for explosive devices, scan automobiles including all entering supply vehicles, and have boat checks. Divers will patrol underneath the pier. We will examine anything that can be looked at beforehand," replied Mr. Tenepior.

Will realized immediately that Mr. Tenepior had once again used one of his most common teaching phrases. The man was so precise.

In his own effort of precision, Will envisioned the commercial. As if the actual image had floated out of the TV screen, he could suddenly see the man from the commercial dropping $7.10 to the ground. "Do you think the attack will be tomorrow?"

Tenepior replied with praise, "We're looking at the details of the commercial just like you showed us. If we read the change he received at the cotton candy stand correctly, then there would only be two possibilities: July 10th which has already passed and October 7th—that's tomorrow."

"What are we going to do?"

"Well, for one thing, you won't be a part of it. I plan on you being safe at the ballpark while we'll be in full force setting up surveillance of the pier. We are planning our counter as we speak."

"Has all that taken into account the Ferris wheel?" asked Will.

"Will, can anyone in the house hear us talking?" Mr. Tenepior cut in.

"No, my parents are downstairs watching the ball game."

"O.K. The Ferris wheel is a possibility, but we believe there is a better possibility of something coming in by boat. The Red Team's main theory involves their contaminating the water or releasing some chemical agent. We'll be sure to check it all out. You just promise me that you'll stay out of harm's way this time."

"I'm not planning on missing this game. Looks like the Cubs will need a win," he replied as he finished the phone call.

Walking back downstairs to finish watching a hopeful, but losing effort, Will felt like there wasn't anything else he could do to help the Red Cell. The experts were well in control. Nothing could happen to the pier with all of their precautions. Everything would be fine.

With a few innings left for the Cubs to stage a comeback, a new sense of purpose, a renewed friendship, a hopeful second chance at a relationship with a beautiful girl he could swear he was in love with, a terrorist attack that would be thwarted, which he had played a hand in, and tickets to a playoff game, his life couldn't get better.

But he had not been the only one sitting down in front of the TV that night. Certain people had been watching the news when reporters questioned a CIA agent discussing the capture of a man supposedly linked to the attack on the Sears Tower. They had also been watching the game for a new commercial and had seen the news flash proclaiming a confession. It definitely had caught their attention. While Will's mind was at ease, theirs were working frantically researching maps and devising plans to strike out, wanting this time to leave a crippling blow in ways Will nor anyone else had thought of.

Chapter 20

Sunday afternoon finally arrived. Will once again found himself at the ballpark with Stacey and Ryan. Will's father had escorted them to the game and taken the seat at the far end of the row as if guarding some possible escape route. Though Will hadn't spoken much to Stacey besides asking her to the game, he thought that this evening would give him time to show her who he really was and break any awkward tension between them.

Stacey, as usual, beat him to the punch. "School was kinda' crazy this week."

Picking up on the comment, Ryan added, "Yeah, that sub on Wednesday was useless. She never did figure out that it was Kyle making those sounds." They all laughed for a second until it became obvious that Mr. Conlan hadn't found it as amusing.

Adding some seriousness to her voice, Stacey said, "Can you imagine what class would have been like on Wednesday if Mr. Tenepior had been there?"

Not wanting to let on that he really knew why Mr. Tenepior was gone, Will said, "Yeah, he'd have probably taken us on a field trip to the Sears Tower. I'm glad he got sick."

"You think he was sick?" asked Ryan. "I would have thought that he'd come to school anyway. I can just hear him now." Copying Kyle's

Tenepior impersonation, he continued, "Suck it up, Girls. You've got to fight through the misery!" Ryan stressed the word "fight" with fake punches to the air.

Once again they burst into a fit of laughter, though Will for some reason felt a little uneasy about the joke.

Mr. Conlan broke in, "Aw, he couldn't be nearly as hard on you guys as my eighth grade science teacher. He had a flat piece of wood on his desk that he used to paddle smart-alecky kids like you. He called it the 'Board of Education.'" Will was used to his I-had-it-harder-when-I-was-younger speech.

Ryan perked up after that comment. "No way. I think Mr. T. was some kind of drill sergeant in the Marines or something." Sinking lower into his green plastic chair, Will's body squirmed to find comfort against Ryan's wild guess.

Stacey revealed, "You must be right. After school that day he assigned you the twenty-five page paper," she paused as Will watched her swallow, knowing she was thinking about the reason he had to write it, "I went back to talk to him about it and right when I got to his door—you're never going to believe this—but through his door window I saw him suddenly slam his fist down onto a desk and break it in half. I've never seen someone swing so hard."

Will had once before shared that very same thought. He was sure that desk had felt the same way Es Sayid had.

"I thought I noticed that we were short on seats," interjected Ryan.

"That wouldn't be why Kyle was moved to the desk beside me?" asked Will.

"Yeah, it was his desk. I forgot that he used to sit in that front seat next to Mr. Tenepior," said Stacey.

For a second everyone was quiet. Will suspected they were all replaying the image of the classroom through their minds.

"So did you end up talking to him?" asked Will.

"After that? Are you kidding me? I figured you'd write the report to keep me alive."

"Yep. I'd even jump in front of a speeding U-Haul." Will had meant the comment to be funny, but it stalled the conversation. The dampening quiet didn't last long as everyone in the ballpark was asked to stand and join in on the singing of the national anthem. Will thought about how Mr. Tenepior was at that very moment protecting all that this song stood for. And he had played a large role in defending it as well.

His silent reverie was ended by the loud deep-recorded blast of, "Let's play ball!" With this call, all nine defensive Cub players ran out to the field to their positions. The right fielder sprinted among the deafening cheers bursting from the curve of the outfield. Digging deep grooves with his feet, the lead-off batter for the Atlanta Braves tapped the corner of the plate with his bat and swung for practice. The Cubs' catcher positioned his glove over the right corner of the plate preparing for the pitch.

When the fastball was called a strike, the batter defiantly shouted at the umpire about the expanded strike zone. Regripping the bat and taking another practice swing, the batter returned to the box. Adjusting his cap, the pitcher reared backward with a high kicking windup and sent an off-speed sinker toward the plate. Swinging, the batter topped the ball, rolling a slow grounder toward second. Running at full speed, the short stop bent low and cast his arm across his sprawling body toward first. Hurrying his throw, the ball soared left of the base. Reaching out with an extended body along the foul line, the gangly first baseman stretched for the catch as the runner safely dove beneath his attempted tag.

Getting to his feet, the runner dusted off his uniform and tugged at his batting glove with his teeth. Stepping four paces off the base, he prepared to run as the pitcher wound up for his next pitch. Kicking out, the base runner lunged toward second. With the shattering of a broken bat, the batter smacked a line drive bouncing through the gap.

Rounding second, the runner raced for third. The fingers of his back pocketed batting glove flapped in his wake as if waving goodbye to the other basemen.

"We'll be lucky to get out of this," interrupted Ryan. With a knowing nod, Will agreed.

The third baseman shifted closer to the line. As if he had heard Ryan's wishes, the pitcher struck the third batter out swinging. The pitcher kicked at the small rounded mound. Will suspected the pitcher could feel all the eyes of the crowd bearing down on him.

On the next pitch, the batter surprised everyone by slapping a bunt. Bouncing several feet down the third base side, the ball rolled right beside the runner dashing to complete the safety squeeze. Catching up to it, the pitcher one-handed the ball to first in time for the second out. To his right side, the runner had slid into home with a shower of dust and gravel filling the air behind him.

"That's not quite how our Will would have played it," shot Ryan with enough sarcasm that Will knew he'd pretty much been forgiven.

Loud boos bellowed from the stands as the pitcher grabbed the rosin bag and slammed it to the ground with a puff of white smoke. A pop-up on the very next pitch ended the inning.

Ryan and Will gave each other a high-five. "That could have been worse," said Ryan with relief.

"Perfect time for a pop-up if you ask me," chimed in Will's dad.

Knowing that the Cubs never made it easy on themselves, Will said, "That's about too much excitement for me." Adding to the nerve-racking play, the first three Cub batters were put down in order.

"We need to slow down and get control of this game," Mr. Conlan muttered under his breath. As if this was the very game plan the Cubs had in mind, the next five innings passed by without even a hit by either team.

Feeling like he needed a change of pace, Will decided to check out the concession stands. "I'm going for a Coke. Anybody want anything?" he asked.

Jumping up, Stacey said, "I'll go with you."

With their long strides, they glided down the cement ramp to the nearest concession stand. Removing his eyes from the walkway, Will glanced sideways at her and said, "I never had the chance to tell you how incredible that foul ball catch you made last game was."

With a smirk she replied, "Think I could make your team?"

"No doubt. We'll have to ask Coach, though. I don't think he's too keen on coaching girls."

Lightly skipping in the air and dancing in front to face him, she grabbed the sides of his hands and said, "I was just kidding. I don't want to play on some boy's team."

Now embarrassed at his proposal, Will gazed at the ground. He kicked at a plastic bottle cap and said, "Oh."

Stacey tilted her head to try to see into his downcast eyes. "That's O.K. I'd rather come and watch you play anyway."

Suddenly feeling as if all the pressures in the world were pulled from his shoulders, Will squeezed her hands back and smiled at her. Reaching the stand, they ordered a couple of small drinks. Glancing up at the TV monitors hanging from the wall, Will could see the Cubs' pitcher was once again in trouble.

The pitcher squinted to make out the upside down fingers marking the catcher's signal. Adjusting the ball for a firmer grip, he threw his slider. For the third time in the game, the batter made perfect contact with the pitch, sending it between the gap in deep center field. As the throw came in, the batter made a lunge for second base, trying to stretch it for a double. With his slide, brown pebbles of dirt rose and thudded against his body. The mitted hand diagonally swatted toward the runner's outstretched hands, but was too late.

With an extra little zip in the next throw, the pitcher sent the ball soaring over the catcher's glove where it rolled to the backstop. Another round of cackles came from the stands as the runner advanced to third. Shaking off the next couple of pitching signals, the pitcher threw a series of change-ups to the outside corner of the plate.

Feeling a tug of his arm, Will noticed Stacey pulling him back toward the ramp to head to their seats. Almost forgetting that they had been holding hands, he now worried she felt like she wasn't getting enough of his attention. Not knowing what to say, he lifted his drink and bit into his straw, gnawing its tip in contemplation of finding the perfect words. Unable to articulate the thoughts that were wound up like the knots in his stomach, he decided it was now or never.

Pulling her to a stop, he caught his breath. With a weightless rise of tingles raiding his stomach, he leaned toward her. Not connecting squarely, he kissed more of her dimple than her lips. With a light head from a disbelieving exuberance, he swayed backwards. Turning her body back with his in the direction of the game, she held him there. Smiling widely, she squeezed in tighter against his side.

The pitcher rolled the ball in his fingers behind his waist until he found the right feel of the threads. Wheeling back with a high kick of his leg, he bore his eyes into the catcher's mitt. Locking his wrist straight out, he flung an off-speed knuckle ball. The batter swung smoothly, catching the ball off the tip of his bat. Snapping with a crack, the ball screamed straight toward the pitcher. Wide-eyed and with a sharp heart-stopping breath, he jerked his glove upward, bracing himself as the ball sank firmly into its pit. Cheers soared from the crowd. Slamming down his bat in disgust, the batter spit at the ground in frustration for making the third out.

To avoid the rush of spectators racing to the bathrooms after the final out, Will and Stacey hurried off to their seats. Though they had just gone for a walk, they enthusiastically stood for the seventh inning stretch. With the high resounding ring of a microphone, actor Bill

Murray, an avid Cubs' fan, cleared his voice and bellowed loud enough so that no one could miss his words, "O.K., Cub fans. Show us what you've got!"

As though a bullet had slammed into his chest, Will staggered backward, falling into his seat and almost pulling Stacey with him. As everyone sang loudly "Root, root for the Cubbies," Will slumped back into his chair with a glazed over paralyzed look on his face. Stacey grimaced at how hard he was now squeezing her hand.

Swirling thoughts kept bouncing back and forth and against each other like the Ping Pong balls of a lottery machine in Will's brain. Images and voices rang out that only he could hear.

*"Just like you taught us. **Show** smoke; let the reader infer fire."*

"We could make him say whatever we want."

"See, Son. That's why you can't let your imagination get the better of you."

"Well, for one thing, you won't be a part of it. I plan on you being safe at the ballpark while we'll be in full force setting up surveillance of the pier."

"If something seems out of place or unusual, question yourself as to the reason why it's there. There has to be a reason the author used it; you just have to figure out why."

Could this possibly be it? Could Will conceivably be thinking that everything they together had planned for, everything the CIA was now doing was completely backwards? The thought that struck him couldn't possibly be right.

"Yah, we'll blow smoke up their…"

It had to be true. The whole CIA team was making a mistake. Everything was going completely wrong. By the time Tenepior's men realized they weren't finding any signs of an attack, it would all be too late. He had to do something.

Letting go of Stacey's hand and turning to his right, he tugged down on the untucked side of Ryan's t-shirt, pulling him into his seat. Stopping mid-line from his singing, Ryan shot him a puzzled and somewhat irritated look. Too lost in his own thinking to notice, Will said into his ear, "Listen to me. I know you won't believe any of this, but you have to trust me. Please promise me that you'll just do what I ask." He worried that precious seconds were ticking away. There might not be any time left.

Ryan shook his head with an oh-please-not-this-again look. Will's mind swirled; random incomplete thoughts came blurting out. Without even taking a breath, Will continued. "Last game. That speeding U-Haul—it was all true—the whole thing. I know this won't make sense, but you've just got to trust me. There's going to be another attack tonight. I know you saw the new Treks commercial. But the CIA is guarding the wrong place." His rambling thoughts came out as mere ranting.

"There's too much to say. I thought we could show smoke with faking Es Sayid's confession on that news flash last night, just like your idea in English class yesterday, and let the other terrorists infer that they would need to run to survive. But then came their commercial. I think they changed plans. Don't you see? It's a snipe hunt! They're not going to attack the pier. They're the ones blowing the smoke. And we inferred the wrong thing!"

Breaking in for the first time, Ryan asked, "We?"

"Tenepior and I. I know that sounds unbelievable, but Tenepior's in on it."

"Man, why are you trying to pull this again? Don't you remember what happened last time you made all this up in your mind? You think Stacey would forgive you again?"

With Ryan's jabbing home the very worst thought that had also crossed his mind, Will suddenly felt as if all the air had been sucked from his life. What would happen if he were wrong? He had barely convinced Stacey to give him this one last chance. Couldn't the CIA handle this on their own? They were trained for it. The last time he acted so irrationally, he about lost everything. "I suppose you're right," he said back to Ryan. "It couldn't be true. Why would they take such a risk, anyway?"

Readjusting his ball cap, he turned his waning attention back to the game. Disgusted at himself for almost blowing it again, he tried to shove all those thoughts to the back of his mind. He wasn't going to take such a risk.

With a chuckle, Ryan leaned over and said, "You know, I may have believed you if you said that Tenepior had been the one driving the U-Haul."

Almost jumping out of his seat, Will stammered, "Oh, Ryan. That's it! That's why they're going to do it. They'll break Es Sayid out! With Tenepior and all of his men guarding the Navy Pier, the Homeland Security substation will be virtually unguarded. That's where they're going to attack!"

Unbelievably, Ryan didn't object to anything he had heard. He merely asked, "What do you need me to do?"

"I need you to get my dad to drive you to the pier and find Tenepior. Tell him that he has to go back to the substation immediately. I'm going to take a cab there now. Do whatever it takes to get them there!"

Rising out of his chair, Will felt a tug on his left arm. Pulling him toward her, Stacey commanded he look directly into her eyes. Realizing instantly that she had heard at least the last bit of their conversation, he knew what she must be thinking. Her pleading eyes spoke the words that were on her mind. And it had been the one reverberating thought through all of this that had been ringing loudest: *I promise I won't do anything crazy this time.*

Chapter 21

Though Will couldn't take the time to fully explain what was going on, he could only hope that Stacey would forgive him again. That disappointing look he had received from her was enough to make him think that she was calling it quits. Even worse, he would have to face his father for running out of the game without an explanation, or worse yet, permission. There was a 100 percent chance his dad would have said "No." He worried that Ryan's loose chatter wouldn't be enough. He hoped they would buy into what he said and would leave the game to find the help he needed. He doubted it. His father would never understand, but Will couldn't do anything about that now.

As his cab approached the address he had given, Will asked the driver not to stop. He knew there would most likely be a lookout, so he wanted to avoid drawing anyone's attention. Squatting down in the back seat, he didn't want to be seen. Looking through the rear window to get a look at the main doors, he asked the driver to slow down. Knowing now that Tenepior had equipped him with many of the same skills he was trained to use as an intelligence agent, Will set his mind to work. Scanning the area looking for anything that might later be of use or would confirm his notion that this was the actual target, he saw two plain black vans backed up to the main doors. Quickly flashing his gaze to the high voltage entry gate, he saw the very clue he had been looking for. The post was absent of any armed guards.

Not wanting to raise any suspicion, he called forward to the front seat, "I think I was off a few blocks. Try driving back around the other side of this building. The house I am going to is somewhere over there." Exiting the car a block away from the artificial home, Will walked to the mailbox that he knew would have a keypad inside. Quickly pressing the four-digit combination he had seen Tenepior use, he exhaled as a sudden slide of the garage door vibrated and rotated upward. Dashing through the opening and around a parked car that had risen up from underneath the ground on the elevator pad, he quickly punched the 5663 code to reverse the doors shut and send him beneath the ground.

Flattening his body against the black metal floor of the car pad as cement walls slid past him, Will scanned the sunken opening passageway for hidden intruders. Spotting no movement, Will recklessly vaulted from the lift before the elevator even halted and raced toward the passageway.

Crouching low, Will jogged down the tunnel until he reached the secret entrance into Tenepior's office. Elevating through the narrow hatchway, he met a burst of light from the main operations hall. Falling to his knees and peering over the wooden desk that shielded him from view, he could make out the forms of six armed men. Es Sayid stood directly in front of the main video screen. His unshirted chest, bound by white elastic wrapping, mirrored other gauzy patches on his neck and face. In a defiant gesture, he stood atop the CIA's eagle-crested coat of arms tiled into the floor as a place of honor.

Targeting a fisted pistol, Es Sayid squeezed its trigger, boring a hole into the whitened drywall a mere five inches above the forehead of a tightly bound and gagged security agent slumped against a corner and packed between three other officers. Pleading eyes stared right back through the bullet's path to the steadied hand of a fully-in-charge Es Sayid.

"You thought you could stop me?" he spat. "Try to put an end to me? I'll just come at you even harder!" For effect, he fired off two more rounds, shattering plaster and dust across their hair and shoulders as they crouched their shaking bodies together.

Es Sayid raised his pistol as he shouted out various commands in a language foreign to Will. Spread out in front of Es Sayid were two pairs of terrorists frantically packing explosive compound and harnessing digital timers to a series of wires. All of the terrorists were dressed in grey coverall suits with various guns slung across their backs. Four separate gym bags lay open on tables. Wires and electronics poked through the tops.

The man furthest from Es Sayid busily strung a detonator cord from an electronic timer and carefully inserted it into a blasting cap. Will guessed that with one wrong move, they'd all be goners. The terrorist carefully maneuvered his fingertips with the precision of a surgeon.

With waves of his gun-fisted hand as if conducting an orchestra, Es Sayid barked more orders. Following the pointed shaft of the pistol, two of the terrorists grabbed duffel bags containing explosive equipment and scurried out of the main operations hall.

Will immediately realized that the terrorists were planning much more than simply rescuing Es Sayid. Computers strewn across the floor were smashed to pieces. A fourth terrorist, whose black growth of beard touched the floor as he bent over, was sifting through the computer wreckage, picking up various motherboards and hard drives. The last of Es Sayid's troops stood guard, holding his machinegun directly at the duct-taped chests of the four gagged men slumped against the bullet-riddled wall.

The gravity of the situation sank into the pit of Will's stomach. Thwarting Es Sayid's rescue was a one-in-a-million chance, but disarming numerous bombs was definitely beyond his capability. He needed help. Help should soon be on its way. If nothing else, Ryan had always been as persistent as a gnat. But looking at those time bombs, Will needed to figure out a way to halt time before the timers were engaged.

Will pondered what could possibly make a terrorist pause what he's doing. He knew a terrorist's ultimate goal was to invoke fear by causing destruction and wondered if he could somehow reverse the psychology against them, but he doubted his ability to find something they were scared of—men capable of suicide bombings weren't frightened easily. They obviously intended to destroy this substation, but he couldn't let them do that just as he couldn't let them destroy Wrigley Field. And then the thought struck him.

Wrigley Field.

The Sears Tower.

Himself.

None of these attacks had succeeded. They had to be a source of embarrassment. The Wrigley letdown had obviously infuriated Es Sayid. And how had they all been outsmarted?

By a class of eighth grade kids.

And if he were a terrorist who had planned and plotted for years, or probably most of his lifetime, and just found out a bunch of kids had been his demise, there was no way that knowledge wouldn't stop him dead in his tracks. In fact, Will was pretty sure it would drive such a person to insanity.

Reaching over his head into the pencil drawer, he felt for the hard-backed leather case containing Mr. Tenepior's iPAQ Handheld PC. Drawing it to his waist and flicking the stylus out, Will poked the screen until he was stopped by a password window. Typing "CIA," "Red Cell," and "Think," his trials failed. Then he pressed the number pad for "5663," and access was accepted. Will couldn't believe that an intelligence agent in the CIA could possibly be dumb enough to use the same password over and over, especially one that wasn't case sensitive.

Scrolling through folders to find media clips of his classroom, he quickly found the dated files. Using the PDA's Bluetooth technology, he leaned around the desk and beamed his program settings to the wireless ceiling-mounted projector in the main operations hall.

Blinking out of sleep mode, the projector discharged colorful rays that formed a squared view of the Sears Tower on the cinema-sized screen and across the shadowed body of Es Sayid. Shielding his eyes with a brow of his hand, Es Sayid turned to face his own outline and surveyed a recent event of smoke billowing beneath an intact fortress. A news reporter was recounting the number of yards the bus had parked away from the entrance of the tower.

Next flashed a live internet broadcast of the Cubs' game still in progress. Fans roared and cheered as those in the left field bleachers tried to start the wave. All appeared to be happily enjoying the game and life. Es Sayid stood transfixed, absorbing the images projecting across his back and screen, his coarse jaw set like the rigid stone his body had become.

Will selected his classroom video for last. As he programmed the iPAQ to showcase, the screen displayed five student-filled rows of desks. A teacher's voice could be heard directing a discussion as students raised their hands. He had specifically chosen the day Ryan tried to make a fool out of him in front of the class. Setting the iPAQ on the corner of the desk, Will pressed the continuous repeat button and dashed to his secret exit. He was certain he had bought his time, but knew the shock would wear off. He needed to be ready when it did.

Chapter 22

Jumping down the flight of steps of the secret entrance, Will devised a plan. He had to reach the substation's electrical source in the underground parking garage and cut the power. Altering the terrorists' ability to see would not only make it difficult for them to carry out their plans, but might also save Will from getting killed.

It was the basis of any covert operation: improvise, modify, adapt, and overcome. Having already improvised with the video clips, Will was now ready to modify the substation's environment with a blackout. Knowing he had seen a pair of night vision goggles that he could swipe from Tenepior's spy collection, he planned to adapt in a way the terrorists couldn't.

Anxious to get to the generators, Will ran beneath the dim florescent luminosity of the narrow corridor at full speed. His mind was focused only on cutting the power to the substation as quickly as he could manage. Sprinting with a confidence that having a solid strategy can give a person, Will wondered if he had truly calculated the situation he was in.

Ahead, Will spotted the murky haze of a digital clock's ominous glow against the wall directly across from the opening of his corridor. He immediately realized that the stark contrast of the greenish glow against the lackluster grey of the passageway's poured concrete walls was a significant change to the underground garage not previously there when he had last vacated it less than ten minutes ago. Fearing for his life, he dove forward to his stomach and thinned his body against the ground.

Assuming that the two terrorists who left the main operations hall had been here and might still be close by, he couldn't let himself get caught. He should have figured out what they were doing with those gym bags. He silently chastised himself for not realizing they'd plant their bombs here as well.

Drawing one hand over the other, he slinked down the rest of the hallway to peer around the corner. An empty canvas duffle bag lay crumpled against the corner just out of his reach. Weighing in that there was absolute silence surrounding him, Will judged the carelessly tossed-aside bag to be a sign of their completed work and departure. He kicked himself up and darted straight across the garage area to the bomb. His shadow cascaded over the timer and its microwave-like programming buttons.

Will observed that the white modeling clay-like bricks were camouflaged in an olive-drab, Mylar-film wrapping and seemed to weigh about a pound each. They had been packed into a rectangular cluster of nine bricks and placed against the structural wall that Will now leaned against. He guessed the timer must have been adjusted to twenty-five minutes as it now read barely seconds more than an even twenty-one.

Never faced before with an exploding device any bigger than a bottle rocket, Will felt beguiled by a youthful fascination as his fingers mesmerized themselves with the cold crackle of the bomb's plastic wrap. Accidently his finger poked through the corner wrapping of the bottom block leaving a thimble-sized dent in the pliable composition C-4 explosive. Will traced the outline of the newly-formed crevice with his fingertip and gauged that within mere minutes it would play its own role in making a crater of this building. Seconds were ticking by.

There weren't enough minutes. How could he do it all? Even if he managed to subdue the terrorists, he'd never make it back in time to deal with the bombs. His plan was falling apart before he even got a chance to carry it out. But his plan was already in motion. The improvised video should still be working its magic.

"Come on, Will. Think!" he said aloud to himself, tensing with the pressure of the fleeting seconds evaporating within his hands. With worry, his eyes scanned the basement and pinpointed the locations of two other bomb clusters. He quickly considered if he would be able to somehow use the bombs against Es Sayid, but decided they'd still destroy the substation either way. Further improvisation was out.

As Will's mind reeled, his eyes fell on the far northern wall squared into the outline of a single garage. In the sole stall was parked the vehicle he had stood against as he came down the elevator shaft. Will had ridden in it before. But that's not what caught his attention. As if it were a divine signal, an upward arrow elevator button bulged from the sidewall, begging Will to grasp its hint. Instantly Will understood a way to modify his predicament.

Not even stopping to consider what he was about to handle, Will ran to the furthest bundle of C-4. He grabbed the packaged compound from its bottom corners and took off toward the vehicle lift. Will hoped that if he could load each bomb in the basement and send it to the artificial house above, time might allow him to stop the rest of the bombs after he was done with Es Sayid and his men.

As Will set the bomb to the iron floor of the elevator, he shuddered at what he had just done. Who knew how temperamental the bombs were? Could he set them off by merely handling them? Stopping in his tracks, Will momentarily paused. Although Will decided no sane person would possibly act this irrationally, it was the very reason it offered the best option. He decided with finality that if the terrorists had carried them in duffle bags, then he couldn't be shaking them any worse. He just didn't know if the timers had already been set when they had made their deposits.

Running to and from the lift, Will deposited the second bomb and hurled himself forward to grab the last. As quickly as he could, he lugged the weighted bundle into his arms and used the wall as a starting block by pushing off with his foot. The extra acceleration caused his foot to miss slightly; the toe of his shoe skipped as it came down to the concrete and sent Will sprawling forward. Fumbling the bomb, Will tried to catch himself with his left arm as he outstretched his right in an attempt to grab the soaring explosive blocks. Instinctively drawing both arms across his head to shield it as he hit the floor, Will expected the blast to strike him head-on. With a dull thud and scraping sound, the bundle landed against the cement. The top edges of the C-4 crumpled in, taking most of the blow. A bottom corner brick broke loose, bouncing end-over-end and breaking open its Mylar-film wrapping.

Rising to his knees, Will reached for the bomb and rolled it over with a push. The flashing pulse of the timer seemed to be changing more rapidly now. Horror struck, Will panicked as he realized that it wasn't just quicker, 20:00 minutes had changed to 19:00 minutes and then to 18:00 with each elapsing real second. Punching the buttons with his fingers, Will tried without success to stop their fast backward countdown. Two more minutes depleted in the split second that Will pressed the third button. He drew back as he realized he'd subtracted even more time.

Mouth gaping, Will frantically jumped to his feet, pocketing the bomb under his left arm and reaching for the fallen brick with his right. Spotting an insane opportunity in his race against time, Will realized that orange-arrowed lift button was a one-way ticket to the quarters above. It had better get moving upwards or these would be his last living fifteen seconds. Beads of sweat swelled across his forehead. Gripping the loose bar of C-4 and packing it into a ball shape between his two hands as he ran forward, Will reared his throwing arm backward and took aim. He had never been a pitcher, but he had made some deadly accurate throws to first base during his shortstop career.

Snapping his wrist forward, the threads spun through the air in a straight line and smacked into the arrow. Mashing itself into the button with the force of the throw, the balled-up compound peeled away from the plastic switch and fell until it met the ascending elevator base. Smoothly rising upward, the lift engaged gears with the hum of any normal elevator. Above, two metal slabs separated horizontally as the lift approached a widening rectangular gap of light.

Will's eyes dared to peer at a horrific flash of ten from the timer as he continued to race forward. As the two floors separated, Will could see a rectangular pit sunk about a foot below the elevating slab. Then his gaze turned to the thick elevator floor swiftly ascending. The Nissan's frame bounced slightly, and a drip of oil from the undercarriage fell evenly between its tires.

Knowing he only had one possibility to make this work, he would have to call on every ounce of athletic training he had practiced for even though, as Ryan would be quick to point out, he had been unsuccessful so many times before. He had already determined it was his only chance.

Opening up his body with the full pumping of his right arm, he harnessed the Play-Doh-like bomb in the pocket of his left arm as if he were racing down a football sideline. In one fluid motion, he cut sideways and kicked out one foot in front of him. As if undercutting a tag, he buckled the other leg underneath and skidded across the floor. Slamming his arm against the metal base of the lift as he skidded past the front opening, Will dunked the bomb onto the ascending elevator floor where it slid underneath the silver car.

Will wished Ryan could have seen that slide; there had never been a catcher who could have tagged him out that time. He pushed himself to his feet. Scrambling away like a bug from a sidewalk crack, he sprinted for the cover of cement barricaded walls near the center of the basement complex. Distancing himself as far away from the lift as possible, he jumped for shelter behind the generator room.

Rolling into a tornado drill posture with his knees pulled to his chest after his fall, Will decided that if the blast didn't kill him, Tenepior probably would. At the same instant, a deafening blast of air and sound slammed all around Will as he imagined the beige-painted house the elevator had ascended into bursting into a fire-lit scattering of splintered wood.

Below ground, a simultaneous burst of gas and energy exploded through the elevator compartment, sending clouds of dust and debris throughout the entire chamber. The eruption of sound pounded his chest like the beat of a bass drum and, for an instant, all air was sucked from his throat. Hundred pound chunks of metal jackhammered themselves into the pockmarked concrete, leaving foot-deep potholes. A jagged half of an alloy wheel skidded past him. Dust swirled about, clouding the entire basement. Seeing his fate sealed, Will realized he had just destroyed his only known safe exit out of the substation.

Chapter 23

Lifting himself and shaking the blanket of dust from his hair and rubbing it from his arms, Will knew he had already reached the moment when his presence here ultimately meant his life was in danger. The shockwave would have jolted the entire substation and alerted Es Sayid and his men. They probably realized now that they had another adversary to deal with. Cutting the power would leave them with little doubt.

Crouching behind the power generators beneath the electric breaker, Will recalled that Tenepior had once said they were kept here so no one would ever tamper with them. With a chuckle Will muttered aloud, "I guess that plan backfired too." Will hadn't been able to resist holding back a creeping smile across his face as he had pulled all the cords from the generators and had lifted both hands through the dust and debris to simultaneously flip all the breakers.

With the sudden wheeze of fleeting electricity and popping flashes of light, the entire building fell to sleep. Visualizing the layout of the passageway, Will ran fearlessly, skidding through two sled-like tracks of dust to a halt beside the revolving darkroom door beneath Tenepior's hidden entrance. Hoping to utilize his only certain advantage of sight, Will raced against time, wanting to catch the terrorists impaired by the darkness.

Flying out the trap door, Will was stopped by a boney shoulder that had embedded itself into the pillow of Will's gut as he was tackled off his feet. Blinded by his own strategy, Will had failed to think through all the dark possibilities. With a straining grunt, someone lifted him off the ground by a fistful of shirt. Will was immediately thrown overhead onto the paper-covered wooden desktop with enough impact to collapse the oak slab and send its varnished legs sprawling outward like road kill. Crashing downward with him came an ink jet printer and two picture frames that narrowly missed his head as they clattered to the tiled floor. Will's right arm fell upon a desk leg that lay atop a ceramic square like an amputated limb.

The darkened figure jumped over the heap of wood to pounce on Will once again. But Will was too determined to let it end that way. Grasping the improvised wooden weapon, he tightened his grip around the cylinder shaft of the desk leg with his right hand. As if splitting a log, Will swung his club head high and sent the leg straight downward at the charging man just as their bodies met. With a crunching thud against his skull and a garbled exhaling grunt, the man's unconscious body flopped on top of Will's hip, momentarily pinning his legs.

Pushing the weight off, Will crawled to the display case of Tenepior's collected spy relics and felt around the second shelf for the night vision goggles. Pulling the Velcro strap past his ears, he unconsciously peered at the man near his feet. Adjusting his eyes to the amplified light of the goggles, Will could see a goose egg shadowed in fluorescent green already forming on the terrorist's forehead.

Will glanced back at the glass-paneled case and considered his options. Reaching in and making note of everything at his disposal, his fingertips brushed over the pointed tip of something sharp. The word "Caltrop" was printed in the bold black lettering on the brass plate. Holding out the baseball sized shiny spiked star, he thought it resembled jacks that he played with as a younger kid.

Further past it on the same shelf was the rounded form of a smoke grenade. Will found it interesting that it would be stored alongside the night vision goggles when smoke grenades would be of little use in the dark. Though he didn't see a use in taking it, for some reason the grenade felt powerful as he picked it up. Knowing he would be up against machine guns, he wasn't about to pass up an exploding device. He then reconsidered the caltrop. It was very sharp, but impossible to carry or hold. He would have to settle on something else.

Loud shouts from at least two men rang out in front of him from the main surveillance hall. With one last hurried look, Will spotted a placard on the next shelf with the printed words "Dead Drop Spike." That sounded promising. Reaching in, he found a hollow capped tube with a sharp point at the end. It resembled the dirt spikes he used to set up his camping tent with at home. Though it wasn't bladed, its sharp point made it the closest thing to a knife he could find. Shoving it in his back pocket, he quickly moved on.

Unable to find anything else that he thought would be useful, even though the cabinet was filled with various objects, he settled on crouching down and picking up the desk leg. As a baseball player, he thought a swinging device would be as well-suited for him as anything.

Chapter 24

Just as he raised the desk leg in his hands, a spray of bullets shattered the glass of the office ahead of him. Throwing his body sideways, he lunged for the cover of the fallen desk. Shards of glass clinked across the floor. Had he been seen? Though he couldn't believe it, it scared him.

Hardly a thing could be made out in the darkness except maybe something white. "My skin!" Will sharply chastised himself under his breath. Having worn only a blue Cubs' jersey to the game, a good portion of his upper body was exposed or whitened with dust. Will thought sharply. Smacking the lid of the inkjet printer, he yanked out the black cartridge. Ducking beneath another spray of bullets, he crawled to the display case. Gripping the caltrop, he smashed open the casing splashing liquid black across his arms. He camouflaged his face with quick slaps of his hands.

He had already lost about forty seconds of his advantage.

Adjusting his goggles and gripping his bat, he charged for the main surveillance hall and slid to his knees just adjacent to the office behind the first row of overturned cubicles. Close to 200 feet across the room stood a gunman who had been guarding the tied-up men with an AK-47 waist high. He shifted his head nervously about in all directions in search of anything his eyes or ears could spot.

Will wondered if his movements could be felt by the gunman as he swayed the gun's tip from side to side in nervous readiness. Intermittently, the gunman fired a few rounds in Will's direction, shattering more glass that rained down from the windows they struck.

Will fingered the safety pin of the smoke grenade. Some of the bullets now were ricocheting closely to him. If he were to succeed, the gunman had to be taken out. Not stopping, the man continued to sporadically fire, forcing Will to stay low to the ground. From his knees, Will would only have half his throwing power. He judged it would be like tossing home from right field. Knowing he had never seen a middle schooler make that kind of throw with perfect accuracy and would never be able to do it from his knees, he did the only thing instinct told him he could do. Yanking the pin and counting to two, he lowered his arm to gently toss the grenade in the air directly above his head. As he released its handle it spun upward in clockwise rolls. Regripping the desk leg, he bore down on the falling metal ball, using the grace of his habitually fluid baseball swing to find its mark.

With a solid smack, the grenade snapped back from the oak in a line drive clear across the long surveillance hall, nailing the man in the center of his gut. A bright burst of billowing smoke heaved out of the turtle-like shell. Falling back more out of surprise than by the force of the object, the man inhaled sharply with the reaction all people have when a sudden flash of terror strikes. It was a breath deep enough to do its damage. With convulsions, he slumped to his side, jerking his hands to his throat. Violently thrusting forward, he spewed a nasty spray of vomit across his bent legs. Uncontrollably rolling about, he coughed and gasped for air. Within seconds his convulsing body fell limp.

Will, jumping up immediately after his swing, ran toward the slumped gunman. Not only wanting to make as much distance between him and his last known location, he needed to free those hostages, though they too had slumped over from the effects of the smoke grenade.

Other than the hissing smoke bomb, the only sound to be heard was his tennis shoes pounding the tiled floor.

Just as he reached the last gray-carpeted row of cubicles, a hardened arm punched outward and clotheslined Will as he ran forward. The collision snapped the strap of the night vision goggles as Will's head snapped backwards and slammed against an overturned office chair. The darkness was blinding.

The steel tip of a boot slashed against the back of Will's calf muscle. Momentarily immobile, Will reached downward for the goggles. Lifting quickly, he peered through the lens to recognize the bomb assembler who was thrusting another kick his way. Rolling slightly to dodge another painful blast, he caused the man to whiff in the darkness. With a lunge Will hurled the goggles across his body directly at the spot where he had seen the man's head.

With a sickening crack, he knew he had found his mark. Seizing his chance, he crawled to his feet and tried to get away. Two giant stone-like hands crunched down on his arm and shoulder, halting him. As he was tugged viciously backwards, Will let a feeble whine exhale from his mouth. In the same motion, he was lifted off the ground and hurled against a paneled cubicle wall, causing it to overturn and fall backwards over another desk.

Grabbing at an office chair, Will tried picking himself up to scurry away, but slipped against loose pads of sticky notes and pens scattered on the floor. Brutally crashing against his back with a shoulder, the man pounced on top of him, restraining him against the ground. As an explosion of air burst from his lungs, Will gave in to the man's overpowering force.

The crack of a fist crushed into Will's cheekbone, sending a cry of pain screaming from his mouth. A swift kick caught Will just beneath his ribcage as the other terrorist, now bleeding from the lip, came to aid Es Sayid in the capture. Together they whipped Will's body over onto his back. Es Sayid sank his knees into Will's biceps, pinning his arms to the floor.

"Why you're that kid," Es Sayid said in a drawling, stupefied voice.

Almost nose to nose, he glared ferociously down with hatred-filled eyes at Will. Adjusting to the dark, Will could make out the toasted crinkles lining Es Sayid's external skin. A row of almost fang-like teeth, ready to rip the flesh from its prey, spat rancid blood-clotted breath that burrowed into Will's nostrils, causing him to choke and wheeze.

Will wanted to answer, but no longer had the strength. Having a swollen tongue and a stiff jaw, he wasn't sure the man would have understood him anyway. Es Sayid screamed in his face, "What happened to the rest of my bombs?"

Raising an unsteady hand, Will defiantly pointed outward with an ambiguous flick of his wrist, and replied wide-eyed, "Boom!" Using the backside of his hand, Es Sayid slapped a stinging blow across Will's cheek.

Will screamed out with the sharpness of pain. "Incinerated. Like your face," Will audaciously sputtered through a thin stream of blood.

Es Sayid sputtered, "How?" He paused and then changed directions. "You think some American school kid's going to stop me?" Clenching his fingers into a fist, he slammed downward, boring his knuckles deep into Will's lower stomach.

"Tie him up next to one of the bombs," Es Sayid ordered the other terrorist. Will felt his body lift with an all-too-easy tug. His feet skittered loosely against the tile as his body was drug to the center of the main operations hall.

With what strength he had left, Will reached out and tried to grasp a sharpened pencil or thumbtack scattered across the floor—anything he could use against his attacker. Thrashing out wildly with his fingers, he grasped at the rounded shapes that rolled through his fingertips, leaving his hands as empty as he guessed his chances were.

With a violent thrust, his body was slammed to the ground. Wincing, Will's arms fell and thudded against something clay-like that rested to his side. The dull thump from his elbow sent an icy chill up his spine as a fluorescent timer shed another important second with an eerie green glow.

"Ah, don't worry. You won't even know what hit you." The man continued to work the rope as a grin stretched across his face. "Unless I explain how this cap's going to trigger a chemical reaction causing these bricks of C-4 to decompose into a variety of gases that will shoot right through you in a shock wave traveling five miles a second. Doubt you'll feel too much pain," the man sneered as he laced the length of rope around Will's back. Pulling the ends back to the front of his chest, he shoved Will's leaning body backward to the floor and rose to his feet to grab more rope.

Knowing there was fight left in him yet, Will thought of the dead drop spike in his back pocket. Remembering its sharp tip, he grasped his fingertips around the hardened tube and threw himself forward at the man's hamstring, sinking the black spike deep into the muscle. Will's falling weight pushed downward on the spike, tearing a wide gash through the back of the man's thigh. With a roar of pain, the terrorist screamed out and dropped to the ground, trying to reach the spike. "Oh, I doubt you'll feel too much pain," Will shot back through clenched teeth as he kicked out and stomped his foot onto the head of the spike, pounding it cleanly through the flesh.

As the man rocked back and forth cradling his injured thigh, Will scrambled to free himself of the rope, kicking it off with maddened thrusts. And then came the click, the click and the cylindrical pressure against his temple that could only mean one thing.

Chapter 25

"Drop what you have in your hands!" screamed Es Sayid.

Will had long ago let loose of the dead drop spike, so he raised his arms and pointed to the man rolling on the ground clutching his leg. With all his racket and thrashing around, the injured man was easy to make out in the dark.

Turning his head back to Will, Es Sayid roared, "You've caused me enough trouble. This time I'm going to make sure it's done right!" Reaching backward and grabbing the malleable bomb, Es Sayid strung the rope around it, tying it to Will's chest. The work was made more cumbersome by the handling of his gun. "Getting in my way seems to be a problem for you."

Will's heart seemed to beat a dozen times to every click of this bomb that he could feel reverberate through his body. His mind raced as to what to do next.

"Don't touch any of those wires. You wouldn't want to speed the timer up any more." Will already knew that this was no lie.

Refastening the rope around Will's waist, Es Sayid secured it with knots to the bomb. Will's vision had adjusted so well to the dark that he could tell Es Sayid was enjoying himself by the delight in his eyes. Will would have preferred total darkness.

Enlightening the situation even more, Es Sayid continued to rant. "The plan was to use this very bomb for a special project at one of your city's greatest attractions. It would have ended the life of thousands. But rarely do I get the chance to meet one of my victims face-to-face. Looks as if I will have to settle on the memory of a boy who meddled in my plans."

Sparing little time in conforming to his new plan, Es Sayid adjusted the timing mechanism secured tightly to Will's chest. In a panic, Will desperately tried to figure out if there was anything he could do. He wondered if pulling a wire would actually disable the bomb. Would it detonate if he pulled the wrong one? Could pulling it also speed the timer up? He wondered how he could have been so stupid to think he could stop this alone.

Will wished Tenepior were here. He knew he'd be able to tear this guy to pieces. The gauze on his cheek was proof of that. He suddenly regretted that Mr. Tenepior taught English rather than self-defense class. Without any lessons of this type, Will judged he might have to resort to kicking, clawing, and scratching. He knew he wasn't above any of it as he longed to tear at the bandage stuck across Es Sayid's face.

Substituting a different type of hurt, Will stung with his words. "The guy who beat you up is the same one who torched your face."

Pausing his fingers from their intricate work and scrunching the one eyebrow left on his face, Es Sayid appeared to be exasperated by what this kid continually was able to do to him. But Will was not finished yet. Calling his shot like the great Babe Ruth, Will gritted his teeth and warned, "And he's my teacher!" Using the momentary distraction to thrust his leg upward, Will forcibly kicked the gun away from Es Sayid's hand.

Will slapped at the ground with his hands like paddles trying in any way he could to distance himself from the aggravated man. The weight of the bomb slowed his frantic escape. Like a lightning strike, a backhand whacked the side of his face again, knocking him to his back. Hurling on top of him, the man gnashed his canine teeth as they combined with his weight to pin Will down. An evil green glare reflected from the man's face as he smiled down at Will.

"You think I need a gun to kill you?"

Es Sayid tilted his head and held his clenched teeth together with a tightening of his jaw. From the fixed expression, Will could tell this was one act that Es Sayid was not going to rush. Pushing his left fist against his own slanted jawbone with four loud cracks of his knuckles, Es Sayid reached down for Will's neck. A satisfied smirk gleaned across his waxy cheek, folding the crusted skin back like bent page corners. Bony fingers clutched Will's throat with the grip of a Marine's handshake, squeezing the life from his soul.

Will squirmed to free himself. He couldn't breathe. His chest was sunken and his throat was sealed. His mouth opened, but no sound came out. His eyes popping, he stared horror-stricken at the face of a killer so filled with hate that he was sucking the very breath of life from him.

Thrusting out, Will beat at the man's back with clenched fists, barely swinging with enough force to leave a bruise. Pulling his legs in and kicking out seeking any possible wiggle room, he flailed about like a baited worm. A push of the man's arms clamped down on his throat even harder. A burning blazed in his lungs as they screamed for air. Pressure popped at his ears and squeezed at the ridge of his nose, tightening the skin across his cheekbones. His throbbing arteries beat at the constricting fingers in their own struggle to push away the hands. Will wanted the hammering in his brain to cease and the strain of the pressure to dissipate or even burst. He wanted to let his shoulders droop with relaxation and let his body sag against the tiled floor. He wanted the ease of soft, caring thoughts to caress their way into his soul.

Summoning flickering wisps of his parents, friends, great ball plays, and Stacey, Will felt euphoria replacing the pressure. This lively tingle awakened his brain, swapping its lethargy for vigor. He couldn't give up. He must have hope. But what could he do now? He pushed at the man and tried to think what he could use to strike back. There had to be something to utilize. There was nothing within reach for his hands to grasp. The spike had surely been his last defense. Searching the darkness, he scanned around him for any possibility.

Time seemed to halt. The flicker of light from the timer paused with an even steady haze as another of the bomb's seconds ticked by. The second lingered as if boasting that it was to be Will's last. In contempt, it seemed to mock him before his very eyes.

He had come so close to stopping all this. And now it was stopping him. Slowly the very last ounce of breath he held desperately onto dissipated as his fingers crumpled open with the relaxing of his hand. Feeling his body lighten and his eyelids flicker shut, his gaze dreadfully relaxed into a dull stare as he wondered how he'd gotten himself into this.

"Man, that kid can think like a terrorist."

The pureness of that thought invaded Will's innate sense of self. With clarity, a reactive force drove against all pure logic. There was no reason for all this; terror was beyond simple rationale. And that's why he was losing. Nothing about this situation was sensible. There was no set of blueprints explaining just how to defeat this evil scheme.

As if this situation were a mere "nine dots" puzzle, Will bent his mind away from assumed rules. Acting as he had so many times before, he knew that boundaries were not always reality and allowed his instincts to extend beyond the confines he wrongly perceived. With a redness now saturating jagged streaks through the whiteness of his eyes, Will gritted his teeth and used his last surge of strength to pull his hand in with a jerk. The buttons were already familiar to his fingertips. Pressing downward with his middle finger, he engaged the timing mechanism depleting the counter of its contents. Rapidly pulsating glows of dying seconds flashed their descent. Staring straight into Es Sayid's eyes, Will grabbed for the man's wrist, clenching it with all his intensity. Fighting against every logical impulse in a body that was instructing himself to fight for freedom, he wrapped his legs into a wrestling hold around Es Sayid's waist.

Doing what no rational man would, Will had in one single moment transformed Es Sayid from predator into prey. He watched as a wave of disbelief flooded across Es Sayid's face. The startled look was accented by the O-shaped outline of his lips. His head shook from side-to-side as if saying this wasn't how people were supposed to act—that people were supposed to be predictable.

Frantically, Es Sayid shoved his throated grip downwards to free himself, but Will, with the courage of a bull rider, dug his heels in deeper. Instantaneous panic flashed across Es Sayid's eyes, questioning what this kid was doing. A cold sweat dripped from a blood crusted crevice in his forehead and glimmered an evil green as it fell toward the rapidly changing numbers.

"No!" he roared, releasing one hand from around Will's neck and frantically yanking at Will's fingers, trying to pry them away. Huffing deep breaths through a gaping mouth, his eyes darted back and forth in a hysterical fit of absolute horror. And in that ironic moment, Will knew that Es Sayid truly felt what it meant to be terrorized.

As if the time bomb had prematurely gone off, an explosion of air burst into Will's lungs. Feeling the weight of the man catapult from his body, Will lurched upward grabbing at his chest. Gulping with all his might at the air around him and violently tugging at the malleable sides of the bomb, he spun sideways to see Es Sayid's body crumpled into a fetal position on the floor behind him, a smoking ooze of blood streaming into the curved crevice of the floor's outlined emblem. The eagle's beak seemed to sip from Es Sayid's defeat. A line of light from an opened doorway poured across the room, highlighting the engraved quote from the book of John encircling Es Sayid's body: "And ye shall know the truth and the truth shall make you free." Gazing back toward the main entrance and through crisscrossing flashlight beams, Will saw the silhouette of a man lowering a pistol to his side.

Loud shouts bellowed from behind him as several soldiers came bounding through, running in all directions to secure the substation. Two grabbed hold of the last struggling grey-outfitted man who was still writhing on the floor.

The attack had been thwarted.

Staring through the haze of floating smoke, Will could see the frame of a solid, sturdy man who only now was allowing his shoulders to droop in relief. Knowing that Ryan had come through for him, Will gazed up at a man who had so earnestly pushed him, used him, and guided him. Knowing that face all too well, he smiled back at his trainer, his rescuer, his teacher.

Chapter 26

Walking along the sandy beach, Will let his eyes follow the wooden outline of the Navy Pier leftward to the Sears Tower standing triumphantly in the distance. Watching the flow of people leisurely strolling its length as they pointed at sailboats and fed the seagulls, Will could feel their easiness. They were not worried or terrified. They ambled without a care in the world, just simply enjoying the cool breeze of a new spring day. Some exited shops with their purchases tucked neatly away in bags. Happy shouts rang out from others enjoying the amusement rides and attractions. Even the faint sweet smell of cotton candy wafted through the air.

Will knew this could have been a drastically changed scene. Not that the buildings or structures were all that important, but because people's lives were. No one could know how many lives were secretly spared or how the way they all lived might have been different, but greatly because of his own cunning and firm reactions, all these people were able to feel the freedom to enjoy themselves.

Since all six terrorists had been apprehended that October evening, not one single successful attack had been carried out on American soil. By risking his own life, Will had not only stopped them from gaining intelligence of their own, but had broken up the entire terrorist cell by deciphering their mode of communication. Though it had been an exceedingly difficult situation to convince his parents that what he had done far outweighed what he had risked, they had embraced him with a surging pride. They were pleased he had done the right thing.

Halting the CIA's strategic teaching operations immediately following the capture of the terrorist cell, Mark Tenepior had been relieved of his teaching duties and replaced with a much more traditional backup. To preserve secrecy, a rumor had been circulated that Mr. Tenepior had resigned to take care of an ailing relative. Only Ryan, Stacey, and Will's family knew the truth.

But that's as far as it went. What they did not know was that Will had secretly never severed his ties to Tenepior. In order to best protect his own safety and the safety of his family, he had secretly continued his work for the agency from his own bedroom computer. Using the latest in communicative software that one day appeared out of nowhere on his desktop, he spent evenings supposedly locked away doing homework, brainstorming creative possibilities back and forth with a man identified only by the numerical ID tag "5663."

Stepping out of the way of a small pointy seashell, Will tightened his grip on the hand he now held in his, letting both hands swing freely with the motion of their pace. Smiling, he considered how powerful human spirit is. He knew those people on the pier trusted they would be safe without even letting a single horrid notion cross their minds.

There once had been imminent danger. Only months before, terrorists, whose whole life missions were dedicated to inflicting fear on the unsuspecting, narrowly missed achieving their goal. Yet here Stacey and he were lazily soaking up the sun and listening to the crash of the waves, walking as easily as if the danger had never scathed their lives.

He filled himself with this knowledge as if taking a deep life-filling breath fueled by the memory of his fight to survive in his last moment of despair. He was content to walk this beach knowing that he had helped restore hope to this American way of life—hope that all America now seemed to embrace. For the girl to his right, Will knew he had finally become a hero.